I0663203

"Hey, Kevin."

"Good to see you, Lisa."

She might not want to see him, but she had to admit he was fun to look at, with his tall frame, well muscled from the years he'd spent doing construction work, and the chiseled features of his face, saved from being harsh by an almost incongruous dimple that appeared when he smiled.

"Good to see you, too," she replied, settling on yet another half-truth.

He gave her a smile that didn't quite match the awareness of her evasion she sensed in his gray eyes. Or maybe she was just projecting her own uneasiness on him. He had this way of making her feel emotionally naked.

Naked…

She was just close enough to catch the clean scent of his skin and imagine that she could feel the warmth emanating from him. Heaven knew she missed being close to a man, but in her experience, the cost for that comfort was more than she was willing to pay.

Dear Reader,

A few years ago I ventured to Davenport, Iowa, for the first time. A very special man in my life was moving there to start a new job. I wasn't exactly inclined to love the place, since it was so far from my home in Michigan, but love the place I did! I visit Davenport—and that special man—whenever I can.

Davenport's lovely neighborhoods nestled along the Mississippi River, combined with its rich history, make it an ideal setting for a Harlequin American Romance novel. It's also perfect for the story of a couple with a lot of history between them. I hope you enjoy the warmth of the village of East Davenport and the growing attraction between harried single mom and bakery owner Lisa Kincaid and maybe-friend, maybe-something-more Kevin Decker. Sometimes love is right in sight; it's just a matter of opening one's eyes!

When your visit with Lisa and Kevin has ended, I invite you to stop by my place at www.dorienkelly.com, or say hello to me on Facebook, where I can be found at www.facebook.dorienkelly.com.

Wishing you all the best!

Dorien Kelly

The Littlest Matchmaker

DORIEN KELLY

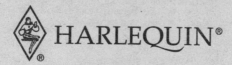

HARLEQUIN®

TORONTO • NEW YORK • LONDON
AMSTERDAM • PARIS • SYDNEY • HAMBURG
STOCKHOLM • ATHENS • TOKYO • MILAN • MADRID
PRAGUE • WARSAW • BUDAPEST • AUCKLAND

If you purchased this book without a cover you should be aware that this book is stolen property. It was reported as "unsold and destroyed" to the publisher and neither the author nor the publisher has received any payment for this "stripped book."

Recycling programs
for this product may
not exist in your area.

ISBN-13: 978-0-373-75284-3

THE LITTLEST MATCHMAKER

Copyright © 2009 by Dorien Kelly.

All rights reserved. Except for use in any review, the reproduction or utilization of this work in whole or in part in any form by any electronic, mechanical or other means, now known or hereafter invented, including xerography, photocopying and recording, or in any information storage or retrieval system, is forbidden without the written permission of the publisher, Harlequin Enterprises Limited, 225 Duncan Mill Road, Don Mills, Ontario M3B 3K9, Canada.

This is a work of fiction. Names, characters, places and incidents are either the product of the author's imagination or are used fictitiously, and any resemblance to actual persons, living or dead, business establishments, events or locales is entirely coincidental.

This edition published by arrangement with Harlequin Books S.A.

® and TM are trademarks of the publisher. Trademarks indicated with ® are registered in the United States Patent and Trademark Office, the Canadian Trade Marks Office and in other countries.

www.eHarlequin.com

Printed in U.S.A.

ABOUT THE AUTHOR

Dorien Kelly is a former attorney who is much happier as an author. In addition to her years practicing business law, at one point or another she has also been a waitress, a bank teller and a professional chauffeur to her three children. Her current (and very romantic) day job is executive director of a lighthouse keepers association.

When Dorien isn't writing or keeping lighthouses lit, she loves to garden, travel and be with her friends and family. A RITA® Award nominee, she is also the winner of a Romance Writers of America's Golden Heart Award, a Booksellers' Best Award, a Maggie Award and a Gayle Wilson Award of Excellence. She lives in a small village in Michigan with one or more of her children and three crazed dogs.

Books by Dorien Kelly

HARLEQUIN TEMPTATION
922—THE GIRL MOST LIKELY TO…
1024—TEMPTING TROUBLE

HARLEQUIN NEXT
OFF THE MAP

HARLEQUIN NASCAR
OVER THE WALL
A TASTE FOR SPEED

Don't miss any of our special offers. Write to us at the following address for information on our newest releases.

Harlequin Reader Service
U.S.: 3010 Walden Ave., P.O. Box 1325, Buffalo, NY 14269
Canadian: P.O. Box 609, Fort Erie, Ont. L2A 5X3

To Kathleen Scheibling. Thanks for the
warm welcome to Harlequin American Romance!

Chapter One

Lisa Kincaid specialized in three things: shortbread, scones and sleep deprivation. She preferred the first two over the third, but as a bakery/coffeehouse owner and single mom of a four-year-old, lack of sleep came with the territory.

"Are you ready?" she called to her son, Jamie, who sat at one of Shortbread Cottage's café tables polishing off his last bits of breakfast. "Miss Courtney's going to think we slept in."

"Ready," he said.

Lisa came around the display counter and checked out his half-finished cup of orange juice. "*Almost* ready."

He grinned, picked up the cup, and then chugged its contents in championship style. When he was done, instead of using the napkin that still rested neatly folded to his left, he wiped his mouth with his hand.

Lisa ruefully shook her head. "Manners, mister."

He pushed away from the table. "Gotta go see Miss Courtney. It's build-a-castle day."

She pointed toward the entry to the bakery's kitchen. "You know where the dishes go."

From her spot at the coffee bar, down at the far end of the counter, Suzanne Jacobs, Lisa's sole employee and all-around lifesaver, said, "I'll take care of it."

Generally, Lisa considered it her duty to womankind to raise a son who could find and use a dishwasher. Today, though, she was willing to cave. It was nearly time for Kevin Decker to arrive for his morning scone and coffee.

Kevin was one of her best customers. Smart man. Great sense of humor. Hardworking. Kind to children and stray dogs…all that good stuff. There were count-less reasons why a woman might want to be in his company, but lately he'd begun to make her feel edgy. Of course it wasn't his fault; Kevin was the same as ever. This was her weird issue. All the same, she needed a for-tifying dose of Iowa autumn sunshine before seeing him.

She took Jamie's hand. "Thanks, Suz. I'll be right back."

"No hurry," Suzanne called over the slow, waking hiss of the espresso maker.

Lisa might have agreed, but Jamie had other plans. As they exited the rambling old clapboard house that served both as bakery and their home, he tugged on her hand.

"C'mon, Mommy."

She smiled as she looked down at her son, who so resembled James, her late husband. Jamie had been not quite a year old when his father had died in an accident.

James never had the chance to see that when his son left infancy, he'd grow to look all Scot, like Aberdeen-born James. Jamie had wild, sandy-brown hair and pale skin prone to freckles. Already, his build was beginning to echo his father's—sturdy and athletic. But her son also possessed her push-on-though determination, as he was displaying right now, practically dragging her down Shortbread Cottage's winding brick pathway in his rush to get to Miss Courtney's Day Care, where he spent weekday mornings.

Three afternoons a week he attended preschool at the rather posh Hillside Academy, courtesy of her parents. It had been a gift Lisa couldn't refuse, much as it had nicked at her pride and independence. But part of being a mom was basing her decisions on Jamie's well-being, not her ego. She could do it, despite the occasional twinge.

When Lisa had become pregnant with Jamie at the age of twenty-one, she'd been shocked and totally unprepared, yet now she couldn't imagine life without him. No longer could she imagine a life away from Davenport's east village, either. Lisa loved the business she'd built for herself in this little wedge of Iowa history overlooking the Mississippi River. Funny, because when she'd been in high school, all she'd wanted was to get the heck out of here. Now she understood that quaint did not necessarily equal boring.

Jamie let go of her hand and began skipping down the sidewalk in front of her. It was the sort of day that made

Lisa want to skip, too. Though it was late September, the air still held the humid perfume of summer and the low, lazy song of a tugboat horn as the vessel pushed its barges fat with newly harvested grain. If she had the luxury of a day off, she'd sit in the park overlooking the river and do absolutely nothing but catch the sun. Okay, not really. Actually, she'd catch up on their endless laundry pile, but a woman should be entitled to her dreams.

"Wait up," she called to Jamie, who was ready to round the corner into the neighborhood that sat behind her home/business.

Jamie danced with impatience, but did as requested.

"So it's build-a-castle day?" she asked once she'd taken his hand again.

Jamie nodded. "Mr. Kevin's bringing over big boxes and we're gonna make a castle."

Lisa slowed. In addition to all the other good stuff about Kevin Decker, he was also her best friend Courtney's oldest brother. Co-owner of a construction company, Kevin had overseen the renovations to the almost crazy-big Victorian that Courtney had inherited from their great-grandmother, making the main floor into the perfect day care center.

"Sounds great," she enthused for her son's sake. For her own sake, she hoped that the build-a-castle plans were slated for later in the day and that she had a few more Kevin-free moments.

No such luck. As they rounded the block, Lisa saw a shiny red pickup parked in Courtney's drive. She didn't need to look any closer to know that Decker Construction was emblazoned on the truck's doors. It was as familiar to her as the white gingerbread trim that Kevin had designed, hand-cut and added to Shortbread Cottage's slate-blue facade last summer.

Kevin's truck bed was already empty of the boxes so there was a good chance he was out back in the play area. Maybe she could escape without seeing him. She felt like a rat for even having these avoidance thoughts.

Jamie chugged up the broad steps to Miss Courtney's covered front porch and then slipped inside without a backward glance at his mother. Lisa followed. As always, Courtney was in the entry hall to greet the children and then send them on to the playroom, where her assistant waited.

Courtney gave Jamie his morning welcome. Lisa was impressed he managed to toss a distracted "Bye, Mommy" in her direction before heading back to the playroom.

"So, what's up?" Courtney asked Lisa. "You two are usually the last in the door."

"I thought I'd shake up my schedule. You know…add a little excitement to my life," she replied while pulling the antique oak front door partway closed behind her.

Laughing, Courtney shook her head, sending her corkscrew blond curls bouncing. "What scares me is that there's a good possibility you're serious. You really are in a rut, you know."

"Rut's too negative. I prefer to think of it as my

beloved routine." Lisa was well aware that she never took time for herself, but she was okay with that. She had to be. Jamie and her business came first.

"Call it what you want, but it's time to give yourself a break. I have an idea…"

Lisa wasn't crazy about the way her friend's voice had taken on the same sort of singsong quality her mother's did when yet another futile dating fix-up was in the offing.

"Ideas are good," she replied in a neutral tone.

Just then another mom and child came in, and Lisa turned to slip out before Courtney pressured her into something she didn't want to do.

"Stay," Courtney commanded.

"I'd rather fetch," Lisa replied, earning a giggle from the little girl Courtney had just greeted.

Courtney gave Lisa a pointed look. "Let's work on stay."

Resigned to her fate, she waited while Courtney chatted with the mom for a second.

After the mom departed, a speculative light returned to Courtney's blue eyes. "Tonight, Kevin, Scott and I—"

Lisa held out her hand like a backup singer. "Stop there. Anything involving three Deckers isn't good…it's dangerous."

"Come on, we're not dangerous."

Lisa thought but knew better than to say *One of you is…to me, at least,* aloud.

"Okay, maybe not dangerous, but definitely a little crazy," she replied instead.

Courtney shrugged. "Guilty as charged, but the least you can do is hear me out."

"If it were another night, I would, for sure," Lisa fibbed. "But Wednesday is Inquisition Night, remember? I have dinner with Mom and Dad."

"That's one heck of a family tradition," a deep voice said from behind her. "What's Thursday, Guilt and Self-recrimination Day?"

Lisa swallowed the panicky feeling that Kevin Decker seemed to bring to the surface in her, then turned to greet him.

He ambled through the front door at the same easy pace he always took, even when at Shortbread Cottage juggling a business meeting over coffee, an incessantly ringing cell phone, and Jamie edging closer to hang out with his favorite customer. While she often had to fake being calm and collected, Kevin appeared to be the real deal.

"Hey, Kevin."

"Good to see you, Lisa."

She might not want to see him, but she had to admit he was fun to look at, with his tall frame, well muscled from the years he'd spent doing construction work, and the chiseled features of his face, saved from being harsh by an almost incongruous dimple that appeared when he smiled.

"Good to see you, too," she replied, settling on yet another half truth.

He gave her a smile that didn't quite match up with the awareness of her evasion she sensed in his gray eyes. Or maybe she was just projecting her own uneasiness on him. He had this way of making her feel emotionally naked.

Naked...

Hot color painted its way across her face as that word invited all sorts of other long-repressed thoughts about literal nakedness to come out and play. And since once freed, they didn't seem to want to leave, she would. Lisa feigned a glance at her watch.

"Well, it's time for me to get back to work," she said.

"I could use my morning coffee. Hang on a second, and I'll walk with you," Kevin offered.

Her gaze was drawn to his long, blue jeans-clad legs and his worn, tan work boots. Feet. She could safely focus on feet, right? Except she'd feel like an idiot, conversing with the man's boots.

"Thanks, but no," she replied. "I really have to run." Which was no lie, even if the motivation for running was messier and more personal than just getting back to Shortbread Cottage.

"Okay, so maybe we can all do something on Friday?" Courtney asked as Lisa was attempting to slip past Kevin and out the door.

She stopped in what was a bad spot—just close enough to catch the clean scent of Kevin's skin and imagine that she could feel the warmth emanating from him. Heaven knew she missed being close to a man, but in her experience, the cost for that comfort was more than she was willing to pay.

"Really, Court, I'm too busy," she said to her friend. "Just have some extra fun for me, okay?"

And then she left before she might recall in any more detail exactly what fun was.

"NOT A WORD ABOUT LISA," Kevin warned his sister after the woman in question had bolted.

Courtney had on her best innocent face, one that he'd stopped buying back when she was sixteen and had "borrowed" his car to take a pack of her girlfriends to a concert in Chicago. Of course, he should have known better than to provide her with a set of keys for emergencies, but that was part of the duties he felt were his as the eldest Decker offspring.

"Why should I say anything?" she asked. "Just because you like her?"

This wasn't a conversation he ever planned to have with Courtney. "Sure, I like Lisa. Who in this town doesn't?"

"No, I mean *like*…like. As in 'Kevin and Lisa sitting in a tree, *k-i-s-s-i-n-g*.'"

He laughed in spite of himself. "You've been hanging around the preschool set too much."

His baby sister stuck her tongue out at him. "Says who?"

"Funny, but here's what I'm saying… Don't push things, okay? I'm capable of taking care of my own life."

"You should be," she said. "Except you're too busy acting like you need to take care of me and Scott and even Mike, who's what…all of two years younger than you? If you were taking care of your own life, you'd have at least asked Lisa out for dinner by now, after all the time you've spent worshipping at her coffee counter."

"Worshipping? It's breakfast."

Courtney took a peek into the doorway to the playroom, probably doing a head count of her charges already there for the day.

"Sure, breakfast at the exact same place every day you're in town," she said as she returned to her spot at the front door.

"She's a friend. That's it. And when it comes to women, I haven't exactly been suffering," he pointed out.

And that was the truth. He dated whenever he wanted to. So what if he'd called a first-date moratorium a few months back? Or was it more like six months ago? Not that it mattered, and not that it was any of his little sister's business.

"You'd be better off looking after your own social life, don't you think, kid?" he suggested.

As soon as he'd said the words, he wished he could yank them back. It had only been six months since she'd broken it off with her fiancé for cheating on her, and rejected the Decker brothers' collective offer to ship him in a storage container to the desolate wasteland of her choice.

Courtney didn't say anything, but he could see the shadows of hurt in her eyes.

"Hey, I'm sorry," he said, before wrapping her in a hug. "I spoke before thinking."

Courtney sighed. "The Decker Curse. That, and wanting the unattainable."

He stepped back and settled his hands on her shoulders. "I don't know about the second part. From what I've seen, we Deckers are pretty good at getting what we want, once we put our minds to it. Don't you think, *Miss* Courtney?" he asked, stressing the *Miss,* since his little sister had fought like a tiger when their parents had balked at the idea of Great-gram's house being turned into Miss Courtney's Day Care, and their only daughter taking on others' children to watch when they wanted grandchildren of their own.

The sadness faded from her eyes. "Yeah, we can be just as tough as we need to be."

The front door opened, and another of Courtney's charges came in.

"You've got me beat, taking on this wild crew," he said to his sister, softening the words with a wink.

She laughed, as he'd hoped she would. "Go on out back and wrestle with your boxes. And, Kevin... thanks."

He knew that she meant for far more than the boxes. Her appreciation of his one or two good traits took some of the edge off not knowing how to deal with Lisa Kincaid's lack of the same.

"Any time, kid," he said, then went to finish his day's work for his sister.

Kevin retrieved his tool pouch and cell phone from his truck's cab. He buckled the well-used pouch around his hips and stuck the phone in its holster. He knew he'd be lucky to go five minutes without a call, and he really could have used some kickoff caffeine.

By now, he'd usually be at Shortbread Cottage having one coffee, black, the scone of the day, and sharing some laughter with Lisa. Courtney was dead-on with that observation; this had been his morning ritual for years, now. But after Lisa's most recent hurried escape, he would skip the scone. He didn't have the stomach for it.

As he walked to the backyard, he checked his phone for missed calls. Four of the six listed were from Scott, his youngest brother and partner. Scott was spending the day at a job site up the river, in Clinton, that was giving them fits. They seemed to be running through a streak of bad luck with subcontractors who couldn't keep on schedule, so Scott was babysitting the drywallers today.

That was the big debate in the construction business— how much work to have performed by direct employees and how much to contract out. After three years with a pared-down crew, Kevin was nearly ready to bulk up on direct employees and deal less with subcontractors, but with the slower winter months coming that would be a bad financial move. Better to wait for the spring. And for a few dark memories to fade a little more.

Kevin opened the safety latch to the backyard's gate, then closed it behind himself. The yard, with its professionally designed playscape, was empty, since the kids didn't come out until just before lunch. At first he'd thought Courtney was officially losing her mind when she'd asked him to stockpile boxes, since the kids already had that marvel of modern architecture to climb through. Then he'd recalled how the empty boxes from his dad's construction jobs had always been the Decker kids' favorite toys. Even though his only steady exposure to kids was a few minutes of Jamie Kincaid's company each weekday morning, he was sure that this part of childhood hadn't changed.

Kevin dragged the appliance boxes, one by one, over to the edge of the playscape area, where the ground was thickly padded with shredded, recycled tires. He pulled the utility knife from his tool pouch, locked the blade into place, and began creating doorways and windows in the corrugated cardboard. He half wished that his life were once again so simple that a pile of boxes could become a castle. But in his world, boxes were boxes and castles were castles. He wasn't sure when the magic had faded. Probably about the time Pop had broken both legs in a fall on a job site. Kevin had been eight and he'd wanted to drop out of school to cover for his dad. Needless to say, Pop had told him to hang on a while longer. He'd ended up waiting until the day after high school graduation.

Sometimes he couldn't believe that sixteen years had

passed so quickly. His dad had cut back to part-time hours in the office about eight years ago, then retired altogether three years subsequent to that. Scott had joined the company after college. It wasn't arrogance to say that they were kicking butt.

But everything in life was about balance, Kevin guessed. On the other side of the scale from that business success remained the truth that his social life wasn't so great, and that he had to bear the burden of the mistakes—financial and otherwise—he'd made since taking over Pop's company. Some mistakes were easier to get past than others.

Kevin paused to survey the boxes he'd altered.

"Almost good enough," he said to himself.

While he was making sure that all rough edges and loose staples had been removed, he glanced toward the playroom. Jamie Kincaid was gazing wistfully out the window. He gave the kid a wave and smiled at the subtle "so teacher can't see me" wave he got in return. He liked the boy as much as the boy's mother had apparently grown to dislike him.

Kevin could name with depressing precision the day Lisa had started looking at him as though he were Public Enemy Number One. That day wasn't three years ago, when, by all rights, she should have started viewing him as a life-wrecker. No, she'd forgiven him the nearly unforgivable long before he'd been able to forgive himself. Instead, she'd started treating him like the village felon a few weeks ago, when he'd made the critical mistake of asking her whether she was feeling okay. Go figure.

He couldn't believe that he was the only person in East Davenport who'd noticed that beneath her smiles and quick humor, Lisa had begun to change. He was perfectly willing to admit he wasn't all that perceptive when it came to the nuances of emotion, so he just didn't get why Courtney and the others couldn't catch the difference. Maybe, though, there was some unwritten rule of platonic semifriendship he'd missed. Maybe he wasn't supposed to acknowledge the lost expression he caught Lisa wearing every now and then. Or maybe he was supposed to buy into that public image she worked so hard to keep in place.

The problem was, he had no intention of following those rules anymore. Something had changed in him, too. Time was that he could look at Lisa and see only the business owner and friend—if she'd ever really been a friend. Their relationship had always been a tough one to categorize.

Now he saw the woman. He saw the sleek, red-brown hair that she kept tied up and wondered what it would feel like to free it. He saw her body's slender curves and wondered how they'd fit against him. And most of all, he wondered if her skin would taste sugary sweet from all her time spent baking. Not that these thoughts were wrong…. He was just flat-out crazy to think anything might come of it.

Kevin took one last look at the boxes and deemed his

job done. He considered just a quick stop at Shortbread Cottage for a coffee for the road, but rejected it. Friday, maybe. He'd try out that old proverb and see if absence would make her heart grow fonder, or at least more tolerant. Assuming she noted his absence. Pushing aside thoughts of Lisa, he jammed his utility knife back into its slot in his apron, then winced at the poke he felt through the thick leather.

"Smart move," he said to himself.

He'd forgotten to sheathe the blade. A quick check after locking it down confirmed that the apron had done its job, and he hadn't managed to stab himself.

Kevin shook his head at his own idiocy. If he didn't get his act together and focus on work, Lisa Kincaid just might be the death of him. And damned if that irony didn't cut more deeply than his utility knife ever could.

Chapter Two

"You're going to need your party manners," Lisa said to Jamie as they pulled up to her parents' house that evening. "Grammie and Grampy have company."

Two strange cars were parked out front on the street. The first was an aged vehicle plastered with the standard assortment of indie rock band stickers and high school cheerleading and volleyball decals—a definite babysitter ride. The other was a sleek sports car, no doubt owned by someone Lisa's parents had duped into being the date candidate du jour.

She pulled past the sports car, which Jamie was excitedly viewing from the elevated perch of his safety seat.

"Pretty," he decreed in a reverent tone.

"Don't get too attached," she said under her breath as she parked her six-year-old and not so very pretty— but paid for—vehicle in the driveway.

Lisa got out of the car and went to the back passenger door to help Jamie out of the constraints of his seat. She glanced up at the house and saw her mother flit by one of the library windows, where she must have been waiting for their arrival. This was definitely a setup; her mother had been wearing a dress. Lisa surveyed her own garb of faded jeans and white short-sleeved top. There would be some severe style clash going down at this meal.

She and Jamie had barely reached the front door when it swung open. Next to her mom stood a perky-looking teenager.

"You're a little late, dear," Lisa's mother said to her before focusing on Jamie. "Jamie, this is Amber. You two are going to have a pizza party in the jungle room."

Mom had this all figured out, down to letting Jamie eat in the glass-walled conservatory, his favorite room out of the many in her parents' home. She could scratch using Jamie as an excuse to bolt.

"Whose sports car?" she asked her mom after Jamie and Amber had left for their pizza safari.

"We're in the living room," her mother replied.

"And?"

Her mother smoothed her hands down her already unnaturally wrinkle-free pale blue linen dress. "And what? Come to the living room and meet the car's owner."

Lisa still balked. "Mom, after last time, you promised you'd never do this again."

"I don't believe I did, and you know I'm very careful with my words."

Which was an understatement. A thirty-year career as a corporate attorney, from which she'd recently retired, had made her mother a tactical genius. In fact,

Amanda Peters, aka Mom, stood among Lisa's pantheon of heroes. She'd managed to work full-time, deal with the fact that Lisa's dad, a physician, worked just as many hours, keep her house so that it looked as though it had sprung fully-formed from a glossy magazine, and still be there for all of Lisa's activities as she'd been growing up. But none of this meant that Lisa had to go willingly onto the merger block.

"Do I have the pizza in the conservatory option, too?" she asked.

Her mother gave an impatient shake of her head. "Oh, for heaven's sake. It won't kill you to socialize a little."

"What do you think I do at work all day?"

"That's not the same thing at all. Now come along."

Because she loved her mom, if not her mom's meddling, Lisa pinned on her smile and steeled herself for yet another awkward dinner.

Her dad and the latest victim were standing at the back windows overlooking her mother's gardens. Lisa held in a laugh as she heard her dad telling the victim that he'd like to put in a putting green. That would happen only if her mom could make it of low-growing thyme, with a lavender border.

"Hey, Dad," she said as she joined them, and then gave her father a hug.

"Lisa, this is Jeff McAdams," her dad said. "He just joined the practice's Bettendorf office."

Which would make it very, very hard for Dr. Jeff to turn down dinner with his new boss. She felt sorry for the guy, especially since between his looks and his career, he was far from the sort to need a setup for a first date. They shook hands and she felt no zing at all, which came as a relief after her encounter with Kevin Decker this morning. She far preferred the feel-nothing mode.

"Iced tea?" Lisa's mom asked her.

"That would be nice." Long Island style—chock-full of liquor—would have been even more helpful.

"So, Lisa, Jeff has just moved here from Ann Arbor," her mother said as she poured tea into a tall, ice-filled glass, then settled a lemon wedge on its rim. "Jeff, Lisa attended the University of Michigan."

They had only reached the credentials stage of Mom's merger negotiations, but it was time to shut down this show.

"I dropped out," Lisa neatly inserted. "No degree and no desire for one. I run a bakery and coffeehouse down in the village. And I have a son, Jamie. He's four. Want to come meet him? He's having pizza down the hallway."

Because Dr. Jeff was the polite sort, even if a little confused by her out-of-the-blue offer, he agreed. Lisa took her tea from her mom and met her exasperated expression with an "outmaneuvered you this time" grin.

"We'll be right back," she said to both parents.

She led Dr. Jeff down the hallway and just outside the conservatory's doors, then stopped.

"I didn't really bring you out here to meet Jamie."

"I had figured as much," he replied.

She laughed. "I don't suppose you could have gotten

through medical school without having a clue, could you? But I know this has to be as uncomfortable for you as it is for me. I'm betting that my father didn't even tell you I'd be here."

"Actually, no, he didn't, but you're not a bad sort of surprise."

While she appreciated the sentiment, it was wasted on her.

"Here's the thing," Lisa said. "You look like a nice guy…in fact, just the sort of guy my girlfriends would tell me that I'm crazy to be giving a quick escape route. But my life is wrapped around keeping my business cranking and being the best possible mom I can be to Jamie. I don't want to date, which is making my mom nuts. I'm sorry you got dragged into this, and I figure we can handle it one of two ways. First, you could stay for a dinner that's going to turn out to be more like a joint interview than a real meal, or you could let me go back into the living room and tell my parents that your pager went off and you had to leave."

He gave her a slow smile. "Do you always talk so quickly?"

"I do when I know my mother's hot on my heels and about to reel you back in. So what's it going to be? Door Number One or Door Number Two?"

He laughed. "Door Number Two."

"Deal," she said, and then just as quickly as she'd separated the good doctor from her mother's plans, she saw him out. Mere moments later, the purr of an expensive sports car departing the area heralded Lisa's return to the living room.

"Dr. Jeff got paged about a patient," she said to her parents.

"Of course he did," was her mother's dry reply. "Now may we have dinner?"

"Absolutely. I've suddenly rediscovered my appetite."

Her father's poorly disguised chuckle didn't sit well with Lisa's mom.

"Don't encourage her, Bob," she said, giving her husband a light nudge before linking her arm through his.

"Then maybe you should stop ambushing the girl."

Lisa followed her parents to the dining room and smiled at their loving banter. Forget the degrees and careers and contributions to the community. For all of her parents' accomplishments, the one that awed her most was that they really, truly loved each other after all these years. If she could pull off that, and only that, she'd feel accomplished, indeed.

Except for the empty place setting in memory of Dr. Jeff, which her mother had declined to let Lisa remove from the table, and for Jamie continuing his safari in the conservatory, their meal followed the course of every other Wednesday. Mom tried to overfeed her, as though there were even a remote chance that while living in a bakery, Lisa couldn't find enough to sustain herself. As usual, Dad talked River Bandits baseball. During the season, she and her dad took Jamie to see as many of the local minor league team's games as they could. The park was a kid-friendly place, complete with a playground, and Lisa loved building these traditions with her son.

With the stuffed chicken breast and spinach salad consumed, Lisa stood to begin clearing the table, but her mother stopped her.

"Let's sit and chat a little as long as Jamie is still having fun with Amber, shall we?"

"Okay." Lisa sat and scrutinized her parents' faces. Mom's was pretty much neutral, but there was something off in her father's expression. Her overstuffed stomach lurched a bit. "What's going on? You're not about to spring something else crazy on me, like a divorce or that I was adopted or something, are you?"

Her mother put one hand to her chest. "Heavens, no!"

Lisa relaxed. "Good. There are some things in life that I need to know won't change."

She watched as her mother gave her father a raised-brow prompt to speak. He didn't appear all that willing.

"Lisa, your mother…well, your mother and I…we wish you'd consider moving back home. We're not saying you should close the business, we just wish you'd give yourself some distance from it. Jamie loves this house, and it's your home, too. You belong here."

"And we could get someone to watch Jamie while you're at work," her mother added. "And of course we'd get him to Hillside for school."

Lisa took a sip of her iced tea to cover her surprise at the course the conversation had taken. Not once, not even after James had died, had her parents suggested she move home. She wanted to ask why the big push now, when she really was back on her feet. But encouraging conversation would leave an opening for her mother, who was a lot more deft and subtle than tonight's attempt at a date fix-up would indicate. If Lisa wasn't careful, she might find herself back in her childhood room, still historically intact with its pink gingham canopy bed and My Little Pony dolls.

"Thanks, but it's covered. Jamie has somebody to watch him, and Courtney does a wonderful job," she said. "She also has a van and driver to get all the preschoolers where they need to be."

"We know, but there's so much we could be doing for you, and for Jamie," her father said.

She knew that, but she didn't want any more of their money. Hillside Academy's tuition she had to swallow for Jamie's sake. She knew what a benefit a fun and early start to education could be. But that was where she drew a big, fat line. She had paid back their start-up loan for Shortbread Cottage as soon as she'd been able to find other financing. Neither did she want them even unintentionally chipping away at her self-confidence. She was feeling strange enough these days as it was.

"I love you both so much and I know that you worry about me, but you don't need to. Really. Jamie and I are fine at Shortbread Cottage. It's our home and we love it."

"But you're all alone," her mother said.

And she'd been achingly alone back when she'd been married, too, but the inner workings of her relationship with James weren't something she chose to share with anyone. He was dead, and his memory deserved to be honored.

"I'm almost twenty-six, Mom, and totally okay with being alone, if you can call it that. To me, it feels like I never have a moment to myself. But my business is doing well, and Jamie is doing all the things he should at his age. You have to know that I'd come home if I felt that his interests were being endangered in any way, but they're not."

"Think about it, at least," her father suggested.

"Okay," she said, but was fairly sure that her parents knew she didn't mean it. And with that, Lisa called an end to Inquisition Night. She wondered, though, if Kevin had been correct. Would she be able to stave off Guilt and Self-recrimination Thursday?

KEVIN, COURTNEY AND SCOTT sat at their usual table in the front window of East Davenport's favorite gathering place, Malloy's Pub. Conal Malloy, a man of many talents, drew the best pint of stout for miles, had a great ear for music and eye for darts, and was one of Kevin's good friends, besides.

Many of Kevin's best nights had been spent in this comfortable place, with its dark wood paneling, glowing old schoolhouse pendant lights, and the sense that one had been sent back in time once inside its door. Tonight wasn't among them. Scott was in a wretched mood after a day of prodding the drywallers to finish up at the

Clinton project. Courtney kept looking at her watch, and Kevin was bone tired, too.

He'd ended the day at the three small homes in slowly revitalizing Bucktown, just outside of Davenport's downtown, that the family was rehabbing with the houses' future owners as part of a community project. Working with amateurs was difficult. He needed to be everywhere at once, making sure that not only was the work being done right, but that everyone was safe.

Kevin looked out the window, thinking it was time to walk home and put this particular day behind him. Just then he saw a little forest-green sedan go by. There were plenty in the area just like it. He knew, though, that this one was Lisa's. The sun had nearly set, but he could still see her features in the dim light. She looked as tired as he felt, and that was saying a lot. He picked up his pint and drained the last of it, then reached for his wallet.

"I need to get some sleep," he said to his brother and sister while pulling out enough cash to more than cover their tab.

"Hang around and listen to the next set with me," Courtney said to Scott when it looked as though he was planning to leave, too.

Scott pushed back his bentwood chair, anyway. "Nah, I really—"

"You really *want* to hear the music," Courtney insisted, using the same emphasis that their mom did when she wished to make it clear that her suggestion was actually a command.

The ploy worked, and Scott sat.

Kevin stood.

"See you at home," he said to his brother. He waved goodbye to Conal, who returned the farewell, and then he ruffled his kid sister's hair just to toy with her a little.

Once outside, he decided to take a moment and enjoy his surroundings. The streets were quiet, as it was both a weekday and after the full push of tourist season, when the Channel Cat ferried visitors across the Mississippi from the Illinois side to fill the village's shops and restaurants. Kevin relished the evening's peace.

He knew what perceptive Court had done, buying him a little time alone before Scott came home. They were currently housemates in a restoration project. Like many of the houses that sat on the hillsides above the village, it was large. However, unlike the rest, they were currently down to two bedrooms, the kitchen, and one bathroom in the way of habitable space. Neither of them was accustomed to such tight quarters. Tonight they'd be like bears circling in the same cramped cave.

Kevin walked uphill, past the old firehouse, and then into Lindsay Park, just the other side of it. Full darkness was beginning to overtake twilight. He sat on one of the park benches overlooking the river. Legs stretched out in front of him, he willed himself to empty his mind of the day's stress and let night come.

He wasn't clear on how long he sat there, as he didn't want to keep time. All he knew was it had been long enough that the lights on the opposite shore now twinkled brightly, and that the village behind him was growing quiet. Kevin rose and began to make his way home.

While there were any number of routes that could have taken him back into the part of the neighborhood where he lived, the most direct was past Shortbread Cottage. Lisa's place sat back on its lot, and she'd made it inviting to customers by putting in a small garden with a couple of café tables beyond the picket fence that James and he had installed just after James had gone to work for him.

Kevin's gaze was drawn to the cottage, but that was no big deal. It was only natural to glance at a place that had been a part of his life for so long. What was a big deal was to see Lisa sitting alone at one of the tables. The lights on either side of the front door and the small solar lights in the garden gave just enough illumination to be sure it was her, but he couldn't gauge her mood.

Kevin figured he could always pretend he hadn't seen her, but that fell far outside of what he considered to be good character in a person. Instead, without slowing too much, he said hello. But he didn't get a hello back.

"Do I strike you as a weak person?" she asked.

That stopped him.

"No," he replied.

"As someone who doesn't have the drive to make it on her own?"

"No."

Even though she hadn't exactly invited him to join

her, Kevin did, pulling out the opposite chair. It felt intimate yet also oddly anonymous, sitting in the dark like this. But if dim light was what it would take to get her to talk to him again, he'd sit there until the sun rose.

"So I take it Inquisition Night was a little rough?" he asked.

"More so than normal. First they ambushed me with a man, and then they asked me to move home. My dad cast the move as being for Jamie's sake, but it felt more personal than that."

Kevin put aside questions about the man ambush, the thought of which bugged him…as did any thought of Lisa dating someone other than him. Instead, he focused on her.

"Jamie seems like one content little guy to me, and I give you huge credit for that. I give you credit for making this place the gathering spot that it is, too. I guess what I'm saying is, Lisa, you're one of the strongest people I know."

She ducked her head, and her hair, which for once was down loose, shadowed her features even more.

"Thank you," she said as her face came back into the sparse light. "Maybe I'm just a little tired. Maybe that's why I haven't been able to just brush off their comments."

"Could be," he said noncommittally. He knew if he told her what he really thought—that to him, she seemed more fragile by the day—she'd be in the house in a heartbeat. "Maybe you need to spoil yourself a little."

Her laugh didn't carry its usual light ring. "I don't think I even know how to spoil myself anymore."

"So, suppose you had a day off, with only yourself to think about, what would you do?"

"Go to the grocery store," she replied without any hesitation.

"You're kidding, right?"

"Hardly. You have no idea what a luxury it would be to shop without a four-year-old in tow."

"So, not a day at the spa or the movies or a bookstore?"

"Afraid not. I'm pretty low maintenance."

He pulled out his cell phone. "It's time for an intervention."

"A *what?*"

Instead of explaining, he did what he did best, and took action. He pushed Courtney's speed-dial number and waited for her to answer. When she did, he said, "Hey, Court, I've got a favor to ask."

"I'd say I'd do anything for you, but I'm afraid you'd ask me to have Scott move in with me. He's a slob."

"Interesting suggestion, which I might take you up on sometime, but no. I was wondering if you would watch Jamie Kincaid tomorrow night? You know, just keep him after hours and give him dinner? I'll pay, of course."

"If you're taking Lisa out, I'll do it for free."

He looked at the woman in question. "I don't know if we're going to have dinner or not. All I know is that I want the opportunity for that to happen."

"So it's not a done deal? Do you even have Lisa's permission for me to watch Jamie?"

"If I don't right now, I will by tomorrow night."

"That's a novel approach, I'll give you that much," Courtney said. "Sure, I'll watch him."

"Great. Love you," he said, then hung up.

He didn't need light to catch Lisa's glare.

"What, exactly, was that about?" she asked.

"It was about getting you to take a breath. I like you, and I don't like what I've been seeing over the past few months. I can't put my finger on it, but you haven't been quite you."

"I don't know what you're talking about."

He knew that she fully understood what he meant, but also saw no point in cornering her. It sounded as though she'd had enough man ambushes for one night. "Then humor me. You close up shop at five, right?"

"Yes."

"Then tomorrow night at six, meet me in Malloy's Pub for dinner. Nothing fancy, not a date…just some talk between two people who could both stand to get out more."

"No!"

"Not so fast, okay?"

"I don't like being railroaded."

He held both hands up in a gesture of surrender. "I'm not railroading you, and mostly because I don't think that's possible."

The stiff set of her shoulders relaxed a little, which gave him hope she wasn't going to walk off and leave him alone in the darkness.

"All I've done is build a window of opportunity, okay?" he said. "Jamie will be happy with Courtney, and you can do whatever you want. Hell, if you want to go to the supermarket and leave me waiting for you at Malloy's, that's an option, too. I won't like it, but I can deal with it."

"Why are you doing this?"

He could still catch an undercurrent of edginess in her voice. "Maybe because you need it. And don't go looking for strings because there are none attached." He stood. "I'll be in Malloy's at six. I really think you should be, too."

He was well past the picket fence when he heard her say good-night. Those words were far from a yes, but at least she was still speaking to him. Kevin felt better than he had in weeks. Now if he could just do the same for Lisa.

Chapter Three

At nearly six the following evening, as Lisa made her way from Shortbread Cottage to Malloy's Pub, one question stuck in her mind: if this wasn't a date, why were her palms clammy?

Maybe she shouldn't have heightened her expectations—and her anxiety level—by changing from her work clothes to a vividly colored sundress, thin cotton wrap and sandals that had a little heel to them. The outfit was undeniably datelike, as was the fact that she had actually put on makeup. While walking to the pub she'd already garnered a teasing comment from elderly Mr. Haughtman, the village's bookstore owner, about being "all gussied up," and a "totally hot" from one of her college-aged coffee customers.

Before opening the door to Malloy's, Lisa drew one last deep and fortifying breath. Maybe she hadn't been out socially with a man other than James since meeting him over six years ago, but she knew she could do this. She just wasn't sure she'd enjoy it.

Lisa stepped into the pub. As always, the place was busy. The mingled scents of garlic and grilled steak wafted from the kitchen, and the chat and laughter of the patrons drifted over the background music. She had just begun to look around for Kevin when someone called her name. She followed the voice to its owner, Kathleen Malloy, sister of the pub's owner, Conal. Kathleen waved her over to where she sat at the bar.

Lisa had known the woman forever. Kathleen, who'd been a few years ahead of her in school and part of the "in" crowd, had become her unofficial big sister when Lisa entered high school. Though their paths had been distinctly different since those school days—Kathleen was now an attorney—they remained friendly.

By the time Lisa had wound through the tables to the bar, Kathleen had stood. The women gave each other a hug.

"I can't believe you're here!" she said. "Pull up a stool and have dinner with me."

"I'd love to, but I'm meeting someone," Lisa replied, then quickly scanned the diners for Kevin. Sunshine streamed into the bar's big front windows, leaving her just the patrons' silhouettes to choose from.

"Is it Courtney?" Kathleen asked. "I bumped into her last night, and she said she's been angling to get you out into the world again."

Maybe it was just a symptom of Guilt and Self-recrimination Thursday, but those "Lisa is a hermit" comments were beginning to sting.

"Hey, it's not as though Shortbread Cottage is a cloistered convent. But, no, it's not Courtney," she said, still glancing around for Kevin.

When she looked back at Kathleen, Lisa noted that she was being scrutinized more carefully.

"I think I have it now," Kathleen said. "You're too dressed up for dinner with Courtney. It's a date, right? But with who? You never get out… You must have tried one of those online dating services and now you have to pick out Mr. Lucky from the crowd!"

Conal, who had just finished waiting on the customer next to his sister, joined in the conversation. "Lisa has a Mr. Lucky?"

Lisa winced. "Ew. That sounds flat-out wrong."

"Lisa's trying online dating," Kathleen advised her brother.

Lisa had seen this game before. The Malloys were like terriers. Once they got an idea clamped between their teeth, there it would stay, fiercely held for their own purposes. In this case, she feared she was the purpose.

"I'm not doing online dating," she said emphatically. "None. Zilch. Zip. Nada."

As she expected, the siblings disregarded her announcement.

"And so we're date-spotting?" Conal asked.

Kathleen nodded her head.

"I'll bet it's the old codger walking in," Conal said as he inclined his head toward an eightyish man. "He's carrying that newspaper so that she'll recognize him.

He'll need it since in his profile he said that he's twenty-eight instead of eighty-two."

Kathleen shook her head in mock dismay. "Damned dyslexia. It'll get a girl every time."

She scanned the room, as did Lisa, though with a different intent. Lisa was pretty sure she'd spotted Kevin at one of the two window tables.

"How about the pierced and tattooed guy at the far end of the bar?" Kathleen asked.

"Nah, that's Harley, and I've been saving him up for you, sis," Conal replied.

Now sixty percent sure she'd spotted Kevin and one hundred percent sure she'd taken enough teasing from the Malloys, Lisa readied herself to move on. "I hate to disappoint you guys, but I'm meeting Kevin Decker, and I think I see him at the windows."

Conal, who'd been quite the actor in high school, ratcheted his performance up a notch to utterly shocked. "You found Kevin on a dating service when he's been beneath your nose all this time?"

"Come on, Conal, you know I didn't find him on a dating service," Lisa said.

Conal grinned. "But you're not denying that you're dating him? Or that you're on one?"

"I'll let you make up your own tale, complete with Irish embellishments, which we all know you'll do, anyway," Lisa said. "See you two later."

"Enjoy," Kathleen said in a cheery—and just a little teasing—voice.

"Take your time, lovebirds," Conal called as Lisa headed toward Kevin. "I'll hold the kitchen open as late as you need. Aren't you glad to have friends in suspect places?"

"Not to mention suspect friends," Lisa replied over her shoulder. Sure as Conal Malloy was the village's most popular bar owner, she and Kevin would now be grist for the village gossip mill.

As Lisa neared Kevin's table, he rose. The nondate had officially begun, and she smiled to mask her nervousness.

"You look beautiful," he said once she'd joined him.

Thank you seemed the most appropriate answer, though she was tempted to add that he looked pretty darned good, too. Kevin always had a neat appearance, which she found surprising considering the rigorous physical nature of his job. Tonight, though, he looked smooth, perfectly dressed in nice jeans and a white shirt. Her fingers twitched with the impulse to touch his freshly shaven jaw. But touching would be even worse than looking, and she was sufficiently distracted already.

"Did you have fun up at the bar?" Kevin asked. His grin rivaled the one Conal had worn.

"I don't suppose you considered coming over there to bail me out?" she asked.

"I considered it, but rejected it. Better that Conal grills me like one of his porterhouse steaks when you're not around to witness my humiliation."

"Somehow I don't see Conal getting the better of you."

He laughed. "Which is why I'll wait until you're not here for my grilling," he said as he held out a chair for her.

Lisa couldn't recall the last time someone had done something this chivalrous for her. In her marriage, chivalry seemed to have been left on Scotland's rocky shore. Not that she was incapable of pulling out a chair or opening a door, but given all that she did for herself and others daily, it was nice to have someone offer to do it for her. Lisa settled in.

"So, did you work up an appetite today?" Kevin asked, then shook his head. "That's an odd question to ask someone who bakes all day, isn't it?"

Could it be that he was a little nervous, too? She liked that idea; it gave her less reason to worry over her every word and gesture.

"Actually, it's not such a strange question," she said. "I have to admit that I'm not much for sweets, but I'm starved for real food by the end of work. And tonight's special because I don't have to think about whether what I want is something Jamie would eat. That's a short list."

He smiled. "You only have to consider yourself. How does that feel?"

Lisa took a moment to inventory her emotions. "Foreign. Even without Jamie here, I find myself craving mac and cheese."

"His favorite?"

She nodded. "Fat grams and carb city. And some-thing I serve only with steamed broccoli to salve my motherly conscience."

"Sounds like a fair deal to me."

She laughed. "Tell that to Jamie."

The waitress arrived with menus, told them about the dinner specials, then asked if they wanted drinks. Lisa ordered a glass of Chardonnay, because she could. Kevin asked for a pint of ale.

"So do your parents ever watch Jamie?" Kevin asked after they'd both looked at the menu.

"Sometimes, but I don't feel right handing him off since he already spends time at Courtney's, plus three afternoons a week at preschool. And now, after last night's talk about having me move back home, I'm even less interested in their help."

The waitress arrived with their drinks. Kevin took a swallow of ale, and then said, "Maybe if you let them help more, they wouldn't push so hard to have you move home. Sometimes you need to let people in just a little, you know?"

While she absorbed what he'd said, Lisa traced a rivulet of moisture coursing down the outside of her wineglass. Maybe he had been speaking in generalities, but she doubted it. His comment had been too much of a bull's-eye. Though she made a point to be friendly and welcoming to one and all, that welcome extended only so far. She'd discovered that she fared better with her boundaries firmly in place.

"I guess that's one way to look at it," she eventually replied.

Kevin looked down at the table, then back at her.

"Hey, I'm sorry. You know, I made a mental list of things I wouldn't bring up tonight, and I've already hit number two on that list. Your relationship with your parents is none of my business, and it's okay to tell me to butt out. It's just kind of second nature for me to offer advice, even when it's not needed."

"So Courtney tells me…constantly," Lisa said, softening her words with a smile.

He grinned. "Figures."

The uncomfortable moment seemed to have passed. She took a sip of her wine, then said, "I know she's an equal opportunity talker. What does she tell you about me? It's a given that I'm a workaholic, but she must have shared something else with you."

He shook his head. "Nope. Can't go there."

"Number one on your list?" she asked teasingly, then realized even before he spoke that number one was James, a topic they both had been tiptoeing around for years.

"Far from it," he said. "It's more about me than you, but just the same, it would be crossing into personal territory. Only mine, in this case."

She nodded as though she understood what he meant, but really, she didn't have a clue.

Kevin gave her a crooked smile, one that barely brought out his dimple.

"I have an idea," he said. "Why don't we take all the pressure off the evening right now?"

She had a laugh at that one. "You do that and you're my hero for life."

"Would you mind standing up?" he asked.

Though she couldn't follow the connection, neither could Lisa see the harm in it. She did as asked. Kevin stood, too, and came around to her side of the table.

Just then the server arrived to take their order.

"If you could hang on for a second?" he asked the woman.

"Sure," she said, and stepped back a few feet, but lingered. Lisa didn't doubt that she was curious. Lisa certainly was.

"We're going to make a brief detour to the end of the evening," he said and then extended his hand.

"How?" she asked, feeling more clueless by the second.

"Trust me." He thrust out his hand a little farther, reminding her that it was there. Because she didn't want to be ungracious, she took it. His grip was warm and firm. She liked the fact that his palm was a little rough with calluses from his work. And she especially liked the way his warmth seemed to be crossing over into her, making her feel bright inside…lit by an exciting sort of vitality she hadn't felt in ages.

"I've really enjoyed my time with you," he said as he shook her hand. "But then again, I always do."

The noise and laughter and even the curious waitress moved so far into the background of Lisa's awareness that they might have disappeared. There was only this man.

"Thank you," she replied.

"I have a confession," he said.

"What is it?"

"Even though I told you that it wasn't, I thought of tonight as a date. And I've wanted a date with you for a while now."

Her heart fluttered in a very, very good way. "Really?"

"Truth," he said with a nod. "You'll always get the truth from me."

Lisa found that more tempting than a promise of yachts and diamonds.

"Okay," she said.

He briefly squeezed tighter on her hand, and the thrill of that warmth again rolled across to her. For all that she noticed their spectators, Malloy's might as well have been a private island paradise.

"Is it okay if I kiss you good-night?" he asked.

She nodded her head in assent.

Kevin leaned forward and gave her a kiss so brief and yet tender that she wanted more. Much more. But with a broad smile and one word—*nice*—he let go of her hand.

"Now that we've gotten out of the way that killer question of how the night's going to end, let's enjoy the evening, okay?" Kevin asked.

Lisa nodded absently. When he pulled out her chair, she again sat. But as she ordered her meal, and as they ate, and even through the rest of their evening's talk—which was admittedly much more fun for having gotten the kiss out of the way—one word haunted her.

Nice.

DINNER WAS OVER, AND THEY were closing the distance to Courtney's house. Lisa, in fact, seemed to be taking on a racewalker's stride, and Kevin wouldn't bet against her arriving there one long-legged step ahead of him.

He knew he'd been taking a gamble by kissing her in the front window of Malloy's. He wasn't worried about the gossip. Hell, he invited it. They were both single, consenting adults, and he preferred that the other guys who hovered around her—not that she ever noticed—believe that the two of them had something going. All the same, he wasn't sure he'd won the gamble. Lisa had relaxed, and he'd managed to keep his foot out of the general vicinity of his mouth for the rest of the night, but it had almost felt as though she hadn't been paying full attention to him. Before, even if she'd been trying to avoid him, he'd been darned certain that she wasn't apathetic toward him.

Courtney's house loomed just ahead.

"You really don't have to walk with me," Lisa said for the second time since they'd departed the restaurant. He had no shortage of self-esteem, but she was beginning to make him worry.

"I know I don't. I just want to."

That slowed her a step. He took advantage of the moment and wove his fingers through hers. She glanced down at their laced hands, but didn't object. If he couldn't coax words from her, he'd figure out what was going on by physical cues. If she still liked him enough to touch him, he remained in the game. Except that this was too personal and too important to him to think of as a game.

"Well, thanks again for dinner," she said when they'd reached Courtney's broad covered porch.

"You're welcome," he replied.

Neither of them reached to press Courtney's doorbell and end the evening. They stood there in silence long enough that the night's first crickets, who had stilled on their arrival, began their song again. Kevin was busy deciding whether he would confuse personal matters more by asking for another kiss when Lisa spoke.

"Here's the thing," she said. "Right now, I want more than nice. It's been a really long time, and I know I'm not being at all consistent, which stinks for you, but nice is like a Sweet Sixteen party, and—"

"Hold on," he said, settling his hands on her shoulders. Her words were tumbling so quickly, one over the other, that it was like climbing his way up a landslide to reach her meaning. "Slow down. What are you talking about?"

"When you kissed me, you said that it was nice."

"And this is a bad thing?"

"Generally, no."

"Generally?"

"I'm not opposed to nice. I mean, it beats the alternative."

Her sense of humor and straight-on approach to life had always made him smile. Tonight was no different. "So what's the issue?"

"I want more than nice," she said again.

She leaned into him, and he could feel his muscles—and another crucial location—respond.

Ah…

Now he understood, and on the most visceral of levels. She sent her right hand up to touch his jaw and then let her fingertips settle beside his mouth, one caressing where he knew his dimple would be, if he were interested in smiling. Right now, there were other things he planned to do with his mouth.

He leaned forward and kissed her once, really more a tease than a kiss.

"Nice is a compliment," he said.

Then he kissed her again, not seeking entry, but allowing his mouth to linger, and damn, but he loved the soft and plump feel of her lips.

"Nice is a *good* thing," he added before briefly kissing her neck.

She smelled exotic, of warm, perfumed places and hot nights, not at all the cinnamon and vanilla he'd always imagined would be her scent. Desire hit him harder than a hammer blow.

"I have to…" he said, but the rest of his thought was too involved to voice. He had to kiss her. He had to know if what he was feeling was real or some illusion that had built up so thoroughly over the years of watching over Lisa that it felt real. He had to do this now, here on his little sister's front porch, of all places.

Lisa watched him almost warily, but she wasn't pushing him away.

"You have to…what?" she asked.

He settled his mouth over hers with real intent this time. Someone's heart was pounding. It might well have been his, but he'd drawn her so intimately into his arms that there was little distinction between the two of them. The soft sound she made—almost a sigh—put Kevin's common sense to bed for the night. He kissed her as he'd wanted to for so long, and it was better and hotter than he'd ever thought to imagine.

She drew back slightly and murmured one word in a sexy challenge. "Nice?"

And then she took the lead in this kiss, going up on tiptoe and demanding that he give as good as he was getting. Kevin obliged, not that he could have stopped himself. It was when he found himself with his hand below the fisherman's net excuse for a sweater she wore, seeking a way to get beneath her dress and touch the sweet curve of her breasts that they both froze.

He disentangled his hand and took a gentleman's step back.

"I, uh…" He had no freaking idea what he was about to say. *I, uh, would do it all again in a nanosecond? I, uh, really should have acted on this sooner…like a year ago?*

No matter. Their eyes still locked even if their bodies were now disengaged, Kevin tried to sort through the emotions he saw pass across Lisa's features as she reached her hand for Courtney's doorbell and firmly pushed it. The night was finished, and judging by the way Lisa's eyes had now narrowed, he was, too.

Chapter Four

What a restless night's sleep couldn't erase, maybe a little hard work would. Though Lisa had been up since five getting a batch of shortbread baking, then readying Jamie for a morning at Miss Courtney's, she couldn't quell the nervous energy running through her. It was now nearly ten, and she still occupied herself with busywork in the kitchen, leaving Suzanne alone at the counter. She couldn't face Kevin today. Not after last night.

Scones had to be the answer. Toffee scones. Sweet, luscious toffee scones. Lisa pulled open the doors to her dry goods storage and looked for the supplies that would lead her to paradise. She could imagine the soft texture, with bits of warm, oozing toffee chips as a surprise against her tongue.

She gave a rueful shake of her head as her mouth began to water. Apparently the passion she'd finally put under lockdown last night was spilling over into her baking. Most days it was a safe bet that selection of a scone flavor wouldn't have her feeling weak at the knees. She needed to pull it together.

"What do you think of toffee scones?" she called to Suzanne through the open doorway to the retail area.

"The same thing I think of all scones. To me they're pretty much the anti-food at this point."

"That's heresy," Lisa said.

Suz popped into the kitchen. "How many scones do you think you've eaten since opening this place?"

Lisa shrugged. "I don't know. Not all that many, really. I sample new varieties, but don't generally snack on them."

"I do, which explains the size of your rear versus the size of mine, and I've only been here a year. You have willpower," Suz decreed, then hustled back out at the cheery chime of the shop's front bell.

Right. Willpower.

Lisa pulled out a stainless steel stool from beneath one of her prep counters and sat. Willpower would explain why last night she'd wrapped herself around a guy who she really wasn't sure she even liked all that much. It would also explain why she'd had to fight herself long and hard to get her hand to the doorbell and end what had been one of the most shockingly hottest kisses of her life. And why, despite knowing it was bad, wrong and stupid, she'd treasure the memory of that kiss for one heck of a long time to come.

"Idiot," she muttered to herself, then went to the sink and washed up. If she concentrated, she'd have just enough time to get a batch of scones baked and cooled before she ferried Jamie from Courtney's to his afternoon of preschool. Whenever possible she tried to do that herself. Those moments with him always made the afternoon fly by.

The scones were in the oven when Suz called from the front, "Lisa, you've got a visitor."

Kevin.

Feeling fluttery and a little freaked-out was unacceptable for all the reasons she'd drilled into her head this morning…but she was. She wished she'd had the foresight—and vanity—to have had installed a mirror somewhere back here. But, no. She'd been too stinkin' practical for that.

Lisa looked down at her flour-dusted apron and figured she could at least rid herself of that. She quickly untied it and hung it on a hook. She debated trying for a perky smile, but realized that given her case of nerves, it would come off as manic at best. Then, when she stepped through the doorway, she saw that all of her emotional gyrations had been for naught.

"Hey, Mom," she said.

"Try not to look so thrilled, dear," her mother replied with a dose of her customary dryness.

"Sorry…I'm just a little out of synch today." She came around the counter and gave her mom a quick hug. "What brings you here?"

"Possibly the fact that you're my daughter and I wanted to see you?"

"What, no potential date lurking outside in the shrubbery?" Lisa asked, then took a peek through the front door's glass because she'd been only half-kidding.

Her mom laughed. "I'm far smarter than to try that on your turf. Give me credit for good tactics as well as good intentions. I thought you might have time for coffee and a chat, though?"

"A couple of minutes, for sure," Lisa replied. "But I have a batch of scones in the oven I'll have to pull soon."

"I'll take what I can get."

"I'll assume that includes a cup of fair-trade Ethiopian, then?" Lisa asked, again rounding the counter to grab a mug for her mom and pour her a cup.

They settled in at a café table, sipped coffee and talked for a few minutes about the civic development group her mom had recently involved herself in, and how excited Lisa was to see two new shops about to open here in the east village. Times had been tough, so each bit of growth was cause for major celebration.

"And where is the world's most wonderful grandson right now?" her mom asked.

"He's at Courtney's, but I have to take him over to Hillside after his lunch."

"Oh, I can do that! Or better yet, we could let him skip school for the day and I'll take him shopping!"

"Mom, Jamie totally loves preschool. He'd much rather be there than out shopping." She wasn't even going to go into the utter uncoolness of introducing the concept of "skipping" to a boy who hadn't yet set foot in a kindergarten classroom.

"I don't know, honey. I think he'd have fun. We could make a run to the toy store, and—"

"No," Lisa said firmly. "You've already bought him every toy out there. He has his own toy room at your house, and it's bigger than my old bedroom."

"But he doesn't have very much here," her mom said, wrinkling her nose in an expression that looked a little too close to distaste for Lisa's already tender ego.

"Yes, I agree that space is limited when compared to your house, but he has what he loves and what he needs."

"It's *home,* Lisa. Your home, too."

Lisa glanced toward the kitchen, then rose. "Gotta pull the scones." And maybe cool down a little, herself.

The three trays of scones were safely on the counter and Lisa's irritation once again at bay when her mom stepped into the kitchen.

"What kind are those? They smell heavenly."

"Thanks. They're toffee." As her mom approached the cooling baked goods, Lisa debated the fine balance between complying with health codes and her personal rules about the kitchen being off-limits, and not offending one's mother. "Why don't we go back out to our coffee?"

"How many scones do you sell in a week?" her mother asked, apparently disregarding the suggestion.

"As many as I can bake," Lisa replied. Scones were trickier to fit into her schedule than shortbread, which was hardier and kept truly fresh for more than a day.

"You should consider contracting out the baking," her mom said, pulling open the refrigerator and peering inside.

"Sure, except for the fact that this is a bakery. People kind of expect me to do my own baking."

"I suppose," her mother said absently while closing up the fridge. "But if you contracted out, you could start selling goods in other locations, too. I think there's a real profit potential there. Everyone raves about your shortbread, and these scones smell positively sinful."

Lisa completely bought in on the sinful thing. One sort of hot moment had translated very nicely into another. All the same…

"Thanks, Mom, but I have no ambition to be the newest cookie queen or whatever it is you're dreaming up for me. I want to make my customers feel happy and warm and I want to make enough money so that Jamie and I can be that way, too. End of story."

"I just see all this potential…"

Her mother might have gestured at the room in which they stood, but Lisa felt as though she was the real target of that comment. My issue, she reminded herself. Not Mom's.

"I think it's about time that I go get Jamie," she said.

"Great," her mom replied. "I'll come along."

"Great," Lisa echoed in as cheery a voice as her mother's.

If diplomacy wasn't the ultimate virtue, Lisa didn't know what was.

KEVIN WAS BEGINNING to define a good day at Decker Construction as one in which the brothers Decker weren't in the office at the same time. He loved Scott, of course, and even liked him 99.99% of the time. But when the two of them were trapped in one small office space along with Rose, their office manager, two desks were one too few.

The phone rang. Rose picked it up. While she was greeting the caller, he asked Scott, "Weren't you supposed to be back up in Clinton today?"

"No need," Scott replied. "The drywallers are done."

"You could always go down to Muscatine and check on the remodel."

"Why don't you?" Scott asked. "Don't think I haven't noticed that you've been dumping all of the out-of-town projects on me."

"It's not dumping. It's a logical division of labor. I have more office duties than you, so I should be closer to it." *And have my own damn desk....*

"Kevin, it's your father on the line," Rose said.

He reached out for the handset so he wouldn't have to give up his spot at the desk to Scott, who was prowling the room.

"No way," Rose said. "You come over here and get it."

Rose, who had worked for his dad for years, had more office seniority than either Kevin or Scott. Though she was somewhere in her late sixties—and Kevin had no intention of asking exactly where—Rose had an energy that he sometimes couldn't match. Except for the desk that the brothers shared, this small office was her domain. In exchange, she let them mess up the attached workshop and storage area any way they wished. Actually, Scott messed and Kevin cleaned.

"Playing favorites, Rose?" he asked as he stood to get the phone. As he'd expected, Scott immediately rolled the desk chair over the old black-and-white checkerboard linoleum floor until it was out of Kevin's reach.

"No favorites," she said. "I'm just adding a little sport to the day. Someone has to even out the odds around here, or you're going to win all the time."

He shot her a "thanks loads" grin as he took the phone.

"Hey, Pop. How's life in Carefree?"

"As advertised," his dad replied.

Four years ago, his dad and mom had moved to Arizona after wintering there for several years prior to that. Though it had wrung him dry financially, Kevin had put together a final buyout from the business and sold his own home to make it happen. Both his parents deserved the good life after raising what had been one challenging pack of kids. Carefree was their sort of town—lots of restaurants, lots of activity.

Kevin tended to head down there when the slow work and persistent cold of January in Davenport got to him, then stick until April. He'd do small renovation projects—jobs good for one guy—to keep the cash flowing, and leave Scott to do the same in Davenport.

"Your mother's talking about Thanksgiving," his dad said.

"Already? It's not even October, let alone November."

"I know, but she's got it into her head that everyone

should come down here. Mike's already said that he can't, so I'm counting on you and Court and Scott."

After a stint in the Marines fresh out of high school, Mike had gone on to college, then medical school, and currently was a resident at a hospital across the river in Moline. Kevin barely saw him these days. No issues other than crazy schedules were at play, though.

"I don't know. That's early for me to be heading down," Kevin said. "Any chance you guys could come up here?"

"Too cold," his father said. "It hurts my damn bones. Not that I'm complaining about being alive."

Kevin chuckled. "I didn't think so. Let me see what I can pull off."

"I'm going to offer to buy Courtney a plane ticket, so she's covered. How about traveling with Scott? You two could always make it a road trip together. It could be a good time."

He looked over at his brother, who was currently moving the stacks of paper Kevin had organized this morning.

"That's pretty tight quarters," he said to his dad instead of what he was thinking, which was more along the lines of he'd rather be strapped to the front of a semi than do a road trip with Scott.

"Think about it, okay? And ask your brother, too."

Kevin could hear his mother in the background, calling for his dad.

"I have to run," his dad said. "I think your mom's started me in a yoga class this morning."

That was an image Kevin could have done without. "Right. Okay. Talk to you later."

After he'd rested the phone back in its base, he asked his brother, "I don't suppose you're planning on getting out of that chair?"

"Not until I find the tile bids on the Clinton house."

"You might try the file marked Clinton. It was on the top of the pile before you started looking."

Scott glanced up. "Huh. Didn't see it."

"You didn't look. You just started taking things apart."

Scott's gaze narrowed into clear annoyance. "You know, I'd ask what's wrong with you today, except you've been like that since last night. I heard you slamming around in the living room in the middle of the night."

"Couldn't sleep," Kevin said shortly. "I figured I'd get some work done. The sooner the house is listed, the sooner we can get it sold."

"I'm with you on that, but three in the morning doesn't cut it as a work hour, roomie. And even if you worked around the clock, the house wouldn't be done until the end of winter…as you know. So, what gives? Did you have a bad date with Lisa?"

"Date?" asked Rose from her spectator's spot at her desk.

"It wasn't a date," Kevin replied to both listeners.

Scott grinned, but said nothing, which was a smart move on his part.

Even dead-of-the-night construction therapy hadn't

taken the edge off of Kevin's frustration. Kevin knew it wasn't his job to think for Lisa, and that she'd rip him up one side and down the other if he tried. All the same, even before they'd started kissing on Courtney's front porch, he'd known the ending wasn't going to be smooth. Both of them were too tightly wound these days for it to have gone any other way. And for that very reason, he'd steered clear of Shortbread Cottage this morning. If he needed to sort things out, Lisa did, too.

"Is this Lisa from Shortbread Cottage that he didn't go on a date with?" Rose asked.

"Yup. The one and only Lisa in Kevin's universe," Scott replied.

"How is she?" Rose asked. "I've missed her since James has been gone."

Not a topic Kevin cared to discuss. Life was sufficiently complicated trying to live it in the present. The past needed to stay there.

He feigned a glance at his watch. "I think I'll go do a walk-around on the new bid request in McClellan Heights," he said.

A couple had bought one of the many old mansions overlooking the Mississippi and decided to renovate the beast themselves. Two years into the process, they had determined that the beast was winning the battle and called Kevin. Kevin had worked on a handful of the houses that sat along that road, and he knew how complex they could be. If Decker Construction got the job, winter would be one huge custom carpentry project.

He wasn't hot on the concept of winter in Davenport instead of Carefree, but they needed the business.

"You mean I get to keep the chair, no hassle?" Scott asked as Kevin reached for the door. "Something's definitely wrong with you."

Kevin didn't comment, since his brother was right. Instead, he closed the door behind himself and headed for his truck. The short drive would do him good, as would the time focusing on work and not Lisa. As he pulled away from the office, he immediately felt freer.

On the way to the bid site, he called the owners and asked for their okay to walk around the property before coming inside. When dealing with large renovations, he always liked to get a mental picture of what they'd do for materials storage. They told him that he was welcome to do so, and to come to the front door when he was ready.

A few minutes later, Kevin pulled between the brick columns that stood as sentinels at the end of the drive. One column bore a stone plaque with the street number, and the other, the house's name: Fairview. Up the drive he wound until he reached the crest of the hill and the buff-colored brick home that crowned it. The owners had bought themselves a gem, albeit one currently in need of polishing.

Kevin parked in the drive and pulled out his notepad, measuring tape and pen and took one circle around the large home. His practiced eye told him that the house was in excess of eight thousand square feet.

Probably more, if any part of the basement was finished. The grounds were smoothly landscaped. The only way he could tell that construction was underway was by some of the third-floor windows, where plywood sat in place of glass.

The backyard was steep, as were all along this ridge of land. A few hundred feet below ran River Drive, the main artery to downtown Davenport. Fairview and all of the houses like it sat so far above the road that noise wasn't an issue.

Just the other side of the four-lane street was a long, green ribbon of a park with a bike path, a narrow strip of railroad tracks, the broad river itself, and the Illinois shore far beyond. He could see why those long-ago captains of industry had chosen to build their mansions here. The view alone elevated the owner from a captain to a king.

Finished with his stroll, Kevin returned to the house and rang the bell. When the massive front door swung open, he introduced himself to the Aldens, with whom he'd only talked by phone prior to this. Maya and Stan were middle-aged, energetic and a little rueful that they were in over their heads. Kevin asked if he could have a tour of the rooms they were currently working to complete.

"We'll go top to bottom," Stan replied. "We've been avoiding the third floor altogether, so it's the worst."

They took a sweeping mahogany circular staircase in the main entry to the second floor, then a less showy set of stairs up to the third floor. They entered one of the rooms with plywood for windows. It appeared that Stan had just propped a piece in front of broken glass. He pushed it aside, and light shone in.

"This is going to be my craft room," Maya said. "At least it will be once we have it free of uninvited occupants."

Bird droppings soiled the wide-planked floor. Kevin looked out the window and across to Illinois. Then he glanced at the manicured lawn below. When he did, the past crawled up to seize him. He braced his hand against the window frame as the room briefly bobbed and dipped beneath him.

"Are you okay?" Stan asked.

"I'm fine," Kevin lied.

Stan's cell phone rang. He answered it, then asked whomever was on the line to hang on.

"It's our daughter, from college. If you don't mind, Maya and I are going to step out and take this."

"No problem," Kevin said. The room was sufficiently crowded with ghosts.

The Aldens left, and even as Kevin turned his back on the window with its jagged glass, memories returned.

It was an accident.

Kevin was sure that never before or since that awful day had he uttered an emptier phrase than that one. Lisa's husband had been in the hospital's critical care unit with virtually no brain function, and that had been the best he could work up.

No comfort.

No sympathy.

Just four words delivered with no emotion at all because he'd felt hollow and useless.

James Kincaid had never been a model employee, but few were. Kevin had known that James was prone to be distracted and disinterested. He'd also been one to carry a grudge, and to feel as though he was being singled out when he was being corrected on his carpentry work.

Countless times Kevin had been so damn close to firing him. The only reason he hadn't was that the guy had had a young child, plus a wife working like a fiend to keep a new business afloat. None of that should have been Kevin's problem, but he hadn't wanted to add to Lisa Kincaid's stress level. He'd always liked her, even back when she and Courtney had done their little-kid best to make his teenaged years a challenge, snooping and tattling whenever they got the chance. And so after hiring James just to help his sister's best friend, he'd given the guy one final chance after another.

Then, one humid August day, he, Scott and James had been working at a house about two blocks from this one. One built to the same scale of size and wealth. One with the same sort of steep yard and rolling lawn.

Thunderstorms had threatened, but had yet to roll in. The heat and humidity had the attic space in which they'd worked a sauna. They'd been converting what had once been maid's quarters into a studio for the house's owner.

Headspace had been good, but the room had been narrow, with one large window on the south wall to provide ventilation. Kevin had figured by its size that it had been a decorative piece, with stained glass, but somewhere along the line it had been replaced with a plain double-hung window. No matter. Even though it didn't have a screen and they were inviting mosquitoes in for a snack, they'd kept the window open. They'd needed air circulation, such as it was.

It had been lunchtime, one like any other. They'd just stopped working long enough to wolf down a quick meal and let tired muscles rest. Kevin had been on both James and Scott to keep drinking water. Hydration had been the only thing that was going to get them through the day.

Done with his food, James had muttered something about being too damn hot, and then sat on the sill of the open window, bracing his hands on either side of his legs.

"Gonna hog all the good air?" Scott had teased.

James, who'd been in a pretty good mood all day—for dour James, at least—had egged Scott on by leaning back so that more of him was out the window than in.

"I might take all the air outside, as well," he'd said.

"Get your ass back in here," Kevin had ordered, then unscrewed the top of his water bottle, tipped back his head and taken a long, deep drink. An approaching train horn had wailed, nothing so unusual with the tracks that ran along the Mississippi. Then, on top of the train's cry had come another. Startled, Kevin had swung to look at his brother, but Scott was leaping toward the window. A window that stood empty of James Kincaid.

In shock, Kevin had looked down. James had lain sprawled, unmoving, on the earth below. Kevin had pulled his cell phone and dialed 911, then sprinted down the sets of stairs, out the front door, and to James.

"He didn't make a sound," Scott had kept repeating as he trailed behind Kevin. "Not a sound."

And James never spoke again, either.

At the hospital, Lisa had been collected, if not calm. He'd tried to tell her what had happened, but because he felt numb and scared and sick, all he'd been able to say was that stupid, stupid comment. *"It was an accident."*

James had died that night of his brain injuries. He'd apparently hit a rock just beneath the surface of the green, perfect lawn. Some luck there. Because Kevin was the boss and James an employee under his supervision, Kevin had spent a solid year bearing the full weight of what had happened.

He should have stapled screening into the window frame that day....

He should have physically hauled James's sorry ass from the window the moment he'd sat down....

He should have fired him that morning, as he'd been so tempted to do, when James had been late again....

Should haves.

Kevin had damn near drowned in them until he hadn't even been able to stand himself. And daily, he'd stopped by Shortbread Cottage once Lisa had reopened the place, at first looking for the words he'd wanted to give her that afternoon. The words had never arrived, and he'd begun to realize that all he could do was watch over her.

She'd bounced back with the same single-mindedness she'd always shown. His respect for her had grown, as had his admiration. He'd waited for her to turn on him, to blame him for James's death. Hell, he still took responsibility for it, if not blame. But Lisa had never gone that route. Sometimes he wished she had. He wanted it all out in the open. He wanted it done. But if she wasn't going to raise it, he couldn't.

Maya Alden popped her head back into the room.

"Ready to move on?" she asked.

"Definitely."

Chapter Five

Hillside Academy smelled of old money and new cars. Lisa, who had parked her serviceable sedan in a spot next to some mommy's Jaguar, asked herself again if she was doing the right thing in having Jamie here.

The answer, as uncomfortable as it might be to her, remained yes. She had actually attended Hillside through seventh grade, at which point she had asked to either attend the public school or join the circus as the last social geek to have escaped Hillside alive. Though her mom was a Hillside alumna, even she had seen that it wasn't necessarily the right place for Lisa. Right now, though, the preschool, with its absurdly generous student/teacher ratio and state-of-the-art everything, was where Jamie should be.

"Campus is lovely this time of year, isn't it?" her mother asked as Jamie zigzagged up the sidewalk in front of them, his Spider-Man backpack bouncing along with his animated gait.

"It is," Lisa agreed. The school abutted to a botanical park owned by the city, which made it seem even grander.

"One day Jamie will be having his senior picture taken under those trees," her mom said.

"How about we just think ahead to kindergarten, okay?"

Lisa didn't want to argue, but neither did she want her mom to believe that Jamie staying at Hillside for all of school was a done deal.

"The time goes more quickly than you could imagine."

She couldn't miss the wistfulness in her mom's tone.

"I know," Lisa said. "And I'm glad you have the freedom now to see a little more of Jamie." But not 24/7.

As they neared the lovely stucco and fieldstone building that held the preschool, Jamie turned around to face them, dancing a few backward steps. "Hurry!"

Lisa laughed as her son then spun on his toes and marched to the door. "The king has spoken."

"If you're the Queen Mother, I don't want to think about what that makes me," her mother said in a dry voice.

"Don't worry. There's plenty of room for princesses around here," Lisa replied as they climbed the broad steps to the preschool's front door. And she meant that in more ways than one.

As always, a group of mothers who had already dropped off their children stood to one side of the spacious entry area. Lisa gave them a wave, just as she did every time she was here to drop off Jamie. A couple of the moms waved back, then returned to making their plans for yoga followed by a little shopping or whatever it was that moms with free afternoons did. To Lisa, they were quite an exotic species.

"I'll take Jamie to the cubby room to put away his backpack," her mom said.

"Okay."

While her mom and son were off, Lisa did the socially proper thing and joined the chatting moms, even though she definitely felt like a sparrow landed in a flock of hummingbirds.

"We were just talking about the Thanksgiving pageant," said a mom Lisa knew only as Carrie's Mommy.

"Already?"

"Of course," another mom replied. "The kids will be getting their information envelopes today. It takes massive planning just to get the husbands on schedule. How about yours?"

Husband, she assumed. Lisa raised her ringless left hand. "Single mom."

She preferred that simple statement to the uncomfortable silence that usually followed an announcement of widowhood. It seemed in this case, though, the silence was inevitable.

"What are you going to do about the pageant?" Carrie's Mommy asked.

Was this a trick question?

"Attend?"

"Oh, you don't know, do you?" asked another mother.

Lisa gave the hummingbirds a cheery smile. "It appears not."

"The pageant is put on by the fathers and children as a thank-you to the mothers. It's been that way forever. Maybe you have someone who can step in?"

Lisa didn't want to take this personally, but she was. At the preschool parents' orientation night, she'd realized that she was in the vast minority as a single parent. That hadn't rattled her a whole lot. She'd always been a tad of a nonconformist, even though that had usually been voluntary.

"No biggie," she replied. "I can step in for myself. I play dad just as well as I play mom."

"I'm sure you do," said Carrie's Mommy.

Lisa wasn't crazy about her tone. In fact, it reminded her of her mom's "why don't you just move home, dear?" song. If Carrie's Mommy reached out to pat her hand, she'd be lucky to get her own back.

She glanced away to see her mom and Jamie returning. Saved!

"Gotta go," she said to the hummingbirds. She was sure they'd have a lovely afternoon nectar shopping together.

After Jamie had been dropped off and she and her mom were on their way back to the bakery, Lisa asked about the whole pageant-as-gift scenario.

"Oh, yes. Absolutely," her mom said. "The show is the pinnacle of four-year preschool. More time and planning go into it than into many weddings."

Considering that it was scarcely October, definitely more of both than had gone into Lisa's impulsive nuptuals.

"Back when you were in preschool, your father was pulled right into the competition among the men. He insisted on making your costume himself. You were one of the Native Americans bearing gifts. As I recall your dress was made from some burlap he found at the garden center. Well sewn, though. The man has done his share of suturing."

Now that her mom mentioned it, Lisa semirecalled the scratchy dress.

"What else do the dads do?" She wasn't much for sewing and needed a game plan to avoid the task.

"Oh, everything. They work on the script with the teacher, though I doubt it has changed much since your day. They build the sets and even provide the music. All that the mothers do is show up."

Not in my case, Lisa thought. Tradition was grand, but this one could use a twist. Jamie had no father, but for this event, at least, he didn't need one.

SATURDAY ARRIVED, and Hillside Academy's old money scent was replaced in Lisa's world by that of Shortbread Cottage's white chocolate/cherry scones. Though the bakery and coffee rush didn't start at the crack of dawn, as it did on weekdays, the crowds that arrived by nine o'clock made up for the wait.

As wild as Saturdays were for Lisa, they were placid for Jamie. His day centered on toys and play and chatting up the customers. Her son was undoubtedly Short-bread Cottage's very best ambassador. And while Lisa scrambled to keep up with her divided duties as mommy and shopkeeper, she was thrilled to see Jamie's broad smiles, receive his kisses and keep his wild hair and sticky hands in some semblance of order.

Right now, he sat in the café area with the large, yellow toy dump truck that Kevin had given him for his fourth birthday, making motor sounds. Jamie had immediately fallen in love with the truck. She suspected it wasn't so much the toy as its giver that had captivated him.

Lisa was brewing up some fresh Costa Rican medium roast to refill the vacuum pots she kept for her regulars, who liked to hang out and read the paper and talk. The coffee's scent hung in the air, a rich counterpoint to that of the scones.

"Can I have one?" Jamie asked, pointing to the fresh baked goods.

"May I?" Lisa said, trying for a gentle grammar correction.

"You want one, too, Mommy?"

He'd sounded so excited that she had to agree. "Sure. Come on around to the kitchen to wash your hands, and then we'll have our snacks."

Jamie pushed his truck under the only empty table.

"Why don't we put that back in our part of the house?" asked Lisa. Anytime the toy lingered on the retail floor, she had visions of a customer slip-and-fall.

"No," he said. "I'm saving Kevin's table."

Lisa shook her head. "He probably won't be here today, sweetie. Just bring it on back."

She hadn't seen Kevin since Thursday night. Whether that was a good thing depended on her state of mind at any particular moment. Late last night when she no longer had the press of the day to distract her, she'd buried her head under her pillow as she'd recalled his mouth hot against hers and his hands leaving her hungry for more. Then, she'd wanted him in a very primal way. This morning, under the light of reason and self-preservation, not so much.

"No. Kevin'll be here," Jamie said with absolute certainty. "He's gotta be. He's going to sit right here." Without paying another bit of attention to her request, he rounded the counter and headed back to the kitchen.

"Jamie's right," Suz said from her spot at the register. "No way will Kevin hold off until Monday, since we're closed tomorrow. But if he does, I win the betting pool."

Lisa looked at her regular customers, who were all deep in conversations or the local newspaper.

"Come on, there's no pool," she said. Everyone in the east village knew that Malloy's was the hotbed of gossip, not placid Shortbread Cottage.

Suz laughed. "Okay, I was joking. But Kevin will be here…guaranteed. I've never seen him stay away from your…*scones*…for this long."

Lisa had to smile at her employee's suggestive spin on a pastry.

"Funny, Suz. Jamie and I will be right back out,"

she said, then joined her son at the low kitchen sink for a scrub-up.

They'd just finished singing "Happy Birthday"—the timing trick she'd taught him for truly clean hands—when the bells on the shop's front door jingled. A moment later, she heard a very familiar low and sexy voice asking Suz for coffee, black, and a scone of the day.

"It's Kevin," Jamie announced. "I want my snack later."

"But you need to…" Lisa began saying, but her son had taken off "…dry your hands."

Lisa wasn't feeling quite the same urge to rush out and greet their most recent customer. In fact, she was content to dawdle rather than face the man whose memory had made her hot and sleepless.

She went to the large metal cabinet that held all of her dry goods. It had been ages since she'd inventoried them. The task was fitting since currently her mouth was drier than a twenty-pound sack of flour. She retrieved her inventory clipboard from her desk and set to work…or at least evasion.

A little while later, Suz popped into the kitchen.

"Kevin was wondering if you're going to be out?"

"Wasn't planning on it," Lisa replied.

"Chicken?"

"Prudent."

Suz snorted. "Prudent? Crazy, maybe. Kevin Decker's no risk. Get on out there and talk to him, if your son will let you get a word in edgewise."

"Is Jamie being a pest?"

"If I said yes, would you lose the chicken feathers and get out there?"

"No, I'd have you bring Jamie back to me."

"In that case, I'll tell the truth. It looks like they're having a nice guy-to-guy chat."

"About what?"

Suz grinned. "I didn't know you were paying me to eavesdrop on the customers."

"And I was pretty sure you did it for pleasure."

"Pleasure. Now there's a better *p*-word than *prudent*…or *poultry.* You might try it on for size one of these days."

Lisa laughed in spite of herself. "Quit abusing the boss and go on back out there."

Suz did, but because she was Suz, she also gave a mighty fine chicken imitation on the way out.

Was she being a coward? Lisa wondered. It felt more like holding on to safety, and she was okay with that. She was about to turn back to her inventory when the phone rang. Lisa ignored it.

"Shortbread Cottage," she could hear Suz saying in an abnormally perky tone out front. "May I help you?"

A moment later, her employee was back in the kitchen. "It's for you."

"Is it a phone solicitor?" Lisa asked as she reached for the handset.

Suz ducked her head and made a choked sound.

Okay. Whatever.

"Hello?"

"I'd really like a couple of minutes with you."

Kevin.

She walked to the doorway. Her heart thumped harder when he gave her a wave with his free hand…the one *not* holding his cell phone. Jamie sat opposite him, and Kevin's coffee mug rested in the back of the yellow dump truck. Adorable. Terribly tempting and adorable. She turned her back on the tableau.

"Cute trick calling me, Decker," she said into the phone.

"Desperate times call for desperate measures."

"Desperate. Somehow I doubt that." All the same, she smiled.

"Okay, so I'm overstating the case, but I couldn't come up with another adage on such short notice. Blame it on a caffeine deficit. I haven't been here in a couple of days, you know."

"I had noticed," she admitted.

"Glad to hear it."

She didn't need to turn around to know that he was smiling, too. She could hear it in his voice, along with a sort of sensual awareness that had been missing from her life for so long.

"I could set up camp out here and spend the day," he said. "It would be no great hardship playing with Jamie and eating your food. I'm pretty sure, in fact, that I could outlast you, there in the kitchen."

"Ah, but I can get into the rest of the house from here."

"Nice bluff. You know you'd never leave Jamie unattended."

"I trust you with him," she said automatically.

The realization of what she'd just said immediately staggered her. She *would* trust Kevin, and she didn't trust just anyone, especially with the most precious person in her life.

"Thank you," he replied. "I'm honored. And I'm glad to hear it."

They both were silent for a moment. For her part, Lisa was trying to pull back emotions she didn't want to come out to play. Feeling desire for Kevin was complicated enough.

"I don't suppose I could talk you into sitting outside with me for a few minutes?" Kevin asked. "A little something has come up that I need to talk to you about. While we chat, Jamie and his truck could work on re-landscaping the front plantings."

"A little bad something or a little good something?"

He chuckled. "So if it's bad, you're going to keep hiding in the kitchen?"

"Maybe."

"You know you can't avoid me forever, right?" said a smooth male voice, not from the phone, but from behind her.

Lisa turned to face him and hit the off button on the handset. "I don't want to avoid you. I should, but I don't."

He snapped his phone shut. "That's almost a compliment, I think."

She smiled. "Almost. Now back on the other side of the counter, please."

When she stepped into the front room, Lisa gave Suz a stern look for letting Kevin come near the kitchen, but her employee didn't look in the least contrite. She simply held out her hand for the phone and gave her an "I told you so" grin.

Lisa followed Jamie and his truck out the front door that Kevin was holding open for them. Today's breeze was crisp with the cool promise of autumn. It felt heavenly after the warmth of the kitchen, even if already it was trying to persuade the shorter wisps of hair at her forehead and temples to escape the elastic she'd used to anchor her ponytail.

"You gonna tell her, Kevin?" Jamie asked.

"I told you I'd handle it, buddy," Kevin replied. "You go move some dirt."

Jamie nodded and tromped off into the well-mulched garden.

"I hope he doesn't get down to dirt," Lisa said.

Kevin smiled. "Figure of speech…guy talk, you know?"

She looked dubiously at Jamie, who was using the side of his sneaker-clad foot to bare the earth beneath her cedar mulch. "Four-year-olds are pretty literal."

"I'll fix it. Promise."

No doubt he would. "So what is it Jamie wants you to tell me?"

"In a second. First, let's get what happened the other night on Courtney's porch out of the way."

"I'm not so sure that's possible," she said.

"Me, either. Nor do I really want to. I've missed you, Lisa. I'm not the kind of guy who's good at games. I'm attracted to you and I want to spend more time with you. I think it's time we just get on to wherever we're heading, okay?"

More time together…. It was such a simple request. Lisa wished that her response could be just as simple, but it couldn't. She glanced over at her son before responding. He was still totally immersed in his play.

She took Kevin by the hand and led him closer to the street, so that she could both watch Jamie and have a little space. And because she'd learned never to expect the luxury of time, she'd just spit it all out now…everything that had simmered in her mind since that heartstopper of a kiss.

"Did Courtney ever tell you how I met James?" she asked, gently working her hand free of Kevin's. He didn't seem to want to let go, but after a brief squeeze, did. She stuck her hands into her jeans pockets. Standing on her own was what she did best.

"Is this question going to have anything at all to do with what I just said to you?" he asked in response.

"Yes," she replied, and then added a qualifier of, "eventually."

"Eventually? Good enough, I guess. No, Courtney and I never talked about James too much."

On the whole, Lisa considered that a blessing.

"Okay, then, here goes," she said after looping a now freed lock of hair behind her ear. "We met at a café in Edinburgh while I was in Europe on a summer study program. I was supposed to be in London, but it was August, I was restless, and the Edinburgh Festival was going on."

"The Edinburgh Festival?" he asked.

"Four weeks of plays and music and comedy and art and partying, basically. A girlfriend and I hopped a train, planning to spend the weekend and maybe skip class on Monday, too. Our first stop was a café for a beer. I met James, and that was it. I never went back. I was swept off my feet, crazy in love…all that stuff."

"Romantic."

"Insane," she replied. "I never stopped to think once."

"Not very Lisa-like," he commented.

She smiled. "Not anymore, but remember the ridiculous scrapes that Courtney and I used to get into? Nine times out of ten, I was behind the good idea gone bad."

He laughed. "And we all assumed it was poor Court, and not you. How many times did she get grounded for you?"

"Lots. Those were the days."

She paused for a second, so that she could choose her words carefully. Her relationship with James was something she didn't want to drag into her budding romance—or whatever the heck this was—with Kevin. "Things are different now. I have Jamie, and he comes before everything else."

Kevin frowned, making his features seem momentarily harsh.

"I understand that," he said. "But I also think that

you don't need to sacrifice happiness because you have a son."

"I know… Really, I do. But from here on out, I want to move slowly when it comes to men and dating. I deserve it, and so does Jamie."

Though she'd never admit it to anyone, had she moved slower with James, they would never have married. The thrill would have worn off, and she would have learned about what sort of man he really was. Lisa could never regret her impetuous act because she had received the amazing gift of Jamie, and she couldn't imagine life without him. But all the same, she was now older and, she hoped, at least marginally wiser.

"Moving slowly is okay with me," Kevin said. "So long as we're moving. Lisa, I meant what I said. I like you. A lot, in fact. I like your determination, your sense of humor…the way you taste when we're kissing."

She looked over at Jamie, but he was busy loading chunks of bark mulch into his truck.

"Let's talk about the kissing later, okay?" she asked Kevin in a low voice.

His smile was a little crooked and a lot endearing. "If we can actually do more than talk, I'm all for it."

"That's honest."

"So far as the statement goes, yeah. I'll save the rest for later, when we don't have a small audience, complete with truck."

She took a deep breath and pushed away the anxiety

that seemed to trail after her like a ghost these days. "The rest? There's more?"

He scrutinized her for a moment. Somehow it felt as though he was looking beneath her skin, and the inherent kindness in his eyes didn't lessen her discomfort.

"Okay, I'm catching on," he said.

"What?"

"I'm beginning to understand how your mind works. You're sure there has to be a downside, aren't you?"

Yes, he was catching on, dammit. "I—"

"No denials. I promised you would always have the truth from me, and I meant it."

"Of course," she said, but knew it for lip service, even as she spoke. "It's just—"

"Lisa, whatever *it* is, it's in the past."

He was right, but that didn't make letting go of the doubts any easier. Still, she needed to try, or years from now, when Jamie had moved from toy trucks to graduate school, she'd remain here…the quirky widow who could bake well, was friendly enough, but was so damn lonely that she ached. She craved her independence, but life had to hold a little more than that.

She nodded her head. "Okay. I'll give this a shot."

He smiled. "I'm hoping with time you'll sound less like you've just lined yourself up in front of the firing squad."

She winced. "That bad?"

"Pretty much, which makes me a little hesitant to go into the next topic."

"Which is?"

"Jamie was telling me that he has a Thanksgiving pageant coming up, over at Hillside Academy. I guess it's something the dads and kids put on for the rest of the family?"

She hadn't known that Jamie was aware of the pageant.

"Correct," she said. "I'm going to do double duty as both mom and dad. Nothing new in the Kincaid household."

"Well, here's the thing… Jamie has asked me if I would help."

"You?"

"Hey, is it so shocking?" he asked in what she figured was a mock-wounded tone. "I do have a couple of skills, you know."

She shook her head. "It's not that. It's just that I have this handled. We're fine."

"You are. But maybe Jamie's got something going on at school. Maybe he's taking some grief for having a family a little different than the others'."

Her heart lurched at the thought. "I'm sure he'd tell me."

Of course he hadn't told her that he knew about the pageant….

"Maybe he would," Kevin said, "or maybe not. He's a pretty perceptive kid, and you have been a little stressed lately, you know?"

"It's possible," she admitted, still not comfortable with how well this man knew her.

Kevin inclined his head toward Jamie, who had abandoned his truck and was coming to join them.

"We'll talk about this later," she said in a low tone to Kevin, then gave her son a welcoming smile.

"Hey, pal," Kevin said to Jamie.

Jamie scuffed one foot against the brick walkway and looked up at them expectantly.

"So, Kevin says you've been talking to him about your Thanksgiving show. Did your teacher tell you about it?" Lisa asked.

"Nope. Carrie did."

No shock that a hummingbird-in-training would preshare the news. Maybe Kevin was onto something about Jamie taking grief.

"Jamie, you know I can help with the daddies, right?" she asked. "It doesn't have to be all boys. We don't need to bother Kevin."

"It's no bother," Kevin said.

She ignored him and focused on her son. "I think it's going to be a lot of fun working on the show."

"I don't want you, Mommy. I want Kevin. He builds castles. You can't build a castle."

And she'd thought Kevin's honesty had stung. "Kevin's busy building real houses for people, too. I can—"

He crossed his arms and scowled up at her. "I want Kevin! He said he'd do it."

A crawly, claustrophobic feeling crept across Lisa's skin. Sure, she was willing to date the guy, but not this! It was too much, too fast. She looked to the man in question for confirmation.

"You did?"

"Yes, but I also said that we had to clear it with your mom, right, Jamie?"

Okay, maybe he wasn't poaching on forbidden territory as much as it suddenly felt to her.

"Want Kevin," Jamie said mulishly.

She did, too, but not in this role.

"Look, I know what you're thinking," Kevin said.

"Please stop doing that," she said.

He gave an apologetic shrug. "Sorry, but I do. Please relax. Don't make this bigger than it is. I'll be seeing a lot more of Jamie than I will of you. Slow and easy still, I promise."

Self-preservation compelled her to tell him thanks, but no thanks; she would be both mom and dad. But the thought that Jamie might be feeling as much a misfit at Hillside as she once had outweighed her personal qualms. She looked at her son and then at the man he'd apparently elected to be a stand-in for a daddy. She didn't need Kevin for the job, but apparently Jamie did. And Jamie came first.

"Okay, then. Jamie and I thank you," she said to Kevin with as much grace as she could muster.

With the matter settled to his satisfaction, her son returned to his truck.

"Can you stop over for dinner tonight, and we'll go over whatever information I can get together today?" Lisa asked Kevin. Now that she'd bowed to the inevitable, she just wanted to get the matter dealt with so that she didn't have to think of him in a daddy role.

He blinked, no doubt startled by the quick segue. "Yes, I can. May I bring anything?"

She was so rusty at these social niceties.

"Whatever you'd like," she replied.

His gaze captured hers, and that warm feeling of intimacy returned. He reached out and brushed away a lock of hair that had been tickling the side of her face.

"Oh, I know what I'd like," he said in a low voice. "You."

That, she could handle.

Chapter Six

Kevin liked to think of himself as a clearheaded sort of guy, and most of the time that was even true. But at dinnertime as he walked up to Shortbread Cottage's open gate, his mind felt muddier than the bottom of the Mississippi River. He knew he wanted Lisa in his life as more than his coffee source, but he didn't want her to feel pressured. He also wanted to help Jamie. He felt sorry for the little guy, who so wanted to be like his classmates.

In helping Jamie, he suspected he was setting himself up for a whole lot of additional hassle with Lisa, who was emotionally fragile, even though she'd never admit it. Still, no way would he have turned down the child to make the mom feel better. That would have been dead wrong.

Okay, maybe it wasn't just his mind. Maybe this whole situation was muddy. Kevin didn't believe the old saying about good guys finishing last, but sometimes it was tough for a man with honorable intentions to finish first.

Jamie stood at the bakery door, palms pressed to the glass and truck at his feet, keeping watch. He waved as Kevin approached. Kevin shifted the bundle of goods he'd bought at the downtown farmers' market from his left hand to his right, and opened the door.

"Hi," Jamie said, then scooted his truck away from the threshold.

"Hey, Jamie," Kevin replied while sidestepping the vehicle. "How are you doing?"

"Okay. But Mommy's mad at my toys. She told them to stay in my room."

Kevin suspected that the timing was off for the wooden yo-yo he'd picked up at the woodcarver's booth this afternoon.

"And how do your toys leave your room?" he asked.

The little boy grinned, his smile an echo of his mother's. "Don't know."

Kevin laughed. "Sure, you don't. Does your mom know you're in the bakery?"

He shook his head. "Nuh-uh."

"Well, let's say we go visit with your mom."

Jamie picked up his truck, which looked enormous in his skinny arms. "'Kay."

Kevin followed Jamie through the kitchen, then through another doorway that led into a living room, off of which branched two hallways. The cottage part of Shortbread Cottage was a misnomer. While the house was only one story, it spread out a good, long way. Like a lot of homes in East Davenport, it had been added onto as extended families expanded. The builder in Kevin was always intrigued when he walked into these old places. Lisa was lucky; her home had been added onto with flow in mind.

"Jamie," he heard her call from another room, "did you bring the toys from under the sofa?"

Kevin grinned as he looked at the plump blue piece of furniture in question. He was pretty sure that snooping under it hadn't been on his "to do" list for tonight.

"Lisa?" he called, not wanting her to come out and be startled. "I think Jamie had the sofa handled before he went into the bakery."

She popped out of what he assumed was her son's bedroom.

"Hey… Hi… I wasn't expecting you yet." She glanced at the watch clasped around her slender wrist. "Guess I should have been, though. I'd say come on in, but you already have."

She looked at her son. "Sweetie, could you stick the truck in your room and then we'll go eat?"

"'Kay, Mommy." Jamie hustled off to his room.

She neared, and Kevin caught the scent of that exotic perfume that had gone straight to his libido the last time he'd smelled it. She was dressed casually, yet still dressy, somehow. With her jeans, she wore a light pink sweater that crossed over in front and tied the way his sister's had when she'd been going to ballet class, back when. He had to say he appreciated it much more on Lisa, now.

"I went to the farmers' market this afternoon. Do you ever get there?" He shook his head at his dumb question. "Of course you don't. You're always here."

She nodded. "Pretty much. So what did you bring?"

He reached into the sack and pulled out the bottle of red from a winery up in Clinton. "A local wine. I liked the name."

She reached for it, and their hands brushed. Lisa jumped, then laughed. "Sorry, I'm a little nervous. If Jamie weren't in the other room, I'd have you do that kiss-and-get-it-out-of-the-way thing again."

He smiled. "I'd like that."

"So would I. But for now, let's try that again." This time, she took the bottle and read the label. "Ms. Demeanor. Very cute."

He dredged out the block of sharp cheddar from the organic farmer. "Healthy cheese."

"Borderline oxymoron," she said, accepting it.

"This from a woman who must go through a truck-load of butter a week?" he replied, then reached again, bypassing the yo-yo. "Dessert…but just for you."

She set the wine and cheese on the low coffee table in front of the sofa and accepted the box. "Chocolate truffles?"

"Yes, but they're actually for the bath. Bringing sweets here seemed like a coals to Newcastle thing, and I wanted to give you something that would make you slow down and spoil yourself a little."

"Wow…"

She looked at the ribbon-tied box in her hands, and Kevin wondered if he imagined the pink rising on her skin. It was possible, since he was also contemplating the flush that would come to her as she bathed. Good gift for her, a little rough on his composure.

"Thank you," she said.

He retrieved the last item from the bottom of the bag and held it out. "I have this yo-yo for Jamie, but I thought you'd better decide when or if he could have it."

Lisa's look was nothing short of surprised…and pleased. "Thank you for asking. Feel free to give it to him. It's more portable than a truck."

"I'm not quite sure I understand that," he said as he set the empty bag on the table.

She smiled. "Almost every day, I've had to negotiate the yellow truck out of going to Courtney's. I think it's his favorite toy, ever."

It felt good to hear that. Very good.

Lisa set down the bath truffles and scooped up the wine and cheese.

"Jamie, dinner's waiting. It's time to leave the truck," she called to her son. At his sound of disappointment, she said to Kevin, "Cue the yo-yo."

Jamie came out, but with a good deal of foot dragging.

Kevin showed him the toy. "I got you a little something today. Ever play with a yo-yo?"

Jamie turned it over in his hands. "Nope."

"I'll show you how to use it," Kevin said.

"In a wide-open space," Lisa added.

Jamie ran ahead to the kitchen.

"I hope you don't mind if we eat in the café area," Lisa said. "Jamie and I like to pretend we're at a Japanese restaurant and eat at the living-room coffee table sometimes, but when it's more than us, we use the café."

"No problem," Kevin replied. He was a little tall for ground-level dining, anyway.

After putting the wine and cheese on a countertop, she opened a large refrigerator and pulled out a bowl, then stuck the cheese in the fridge.

"I've made lasagna for dinner. That work for you?" she asked while opening the oven and bending down to peek inside.

"Absolutely. But I'd eat haggis if it meant I could sit across from you."

She closed the oven and stood. "Haggis? Guaranteed that will never happen. We do have a few minutes on the lasagna, though."

"So…do you have a corkscrew in here?" he asked.

"Actually, yes."

While he opened the wine, Lisa went into the café, where he heard her talking to Jamie about nonlethal use of a yo-yo.

"He's all settled," she said as she reentered the kitchen.

He pulled out a stool from beneath a work counter that stood in the middle of the room. With a sweep of his hand, he offered it to her.

"Now it's your turn to settle."

"Thank you," she said.

Once she was seated with her back to the counter, facing him, he handed her a glass of wine.

"I liked listening to you talk to Jamie. You're a good mom," he said.

She took a small sip from her glass, then gave a diffident shrug. "I'm what I have to be."

He wondered how such an amazing woman could seem completely unpracticed in accepting kind words.

"You're more than that, Lisa Kincaid, and I'm betting it's not easy at all," he said.

"Parenthood? No. And single parenthood is definitely not for sissies." She reached to her right and set the wineglass on the counter. "But we're pretty good at what we do, Jamie and I. We're a team. Now, the other parts of my life, they're a little less together. I've decided I need to work on them, for sure."

She had her worried face on. At least, he knew it was her worried face. Court and the others would tell him that he was crazy, that she looked as serene as always. And he supposed she did…to them.

"Are you talking about the more adult parts, maybe?" he asked.

She nodded.

"You're not the only one," he admitted. "What do you say we work on it together?"

He liked that the worry had eased from her features. In its stead were a sparkle in her eyes and a flirtatious curve to her mouth.

"Sort of like study partners?" she asked.

He laughed. "Except this sounds better than any class I ever took."

"I think the lab classes ought to be pretty interesting."

He tilted his head. "Really? What do you think the first lab should involve?"

She hesitated as though mulling the idea over.

"Kissing," she finally said. "Definitely kissing."

His favorite topic. He leaned in until he could have easily settled his mouth over hers for the kiss he planned to claim.

"You sure?" he teased, just a fraction of an inch from paradise.

"Practice makes perfect." She brought her lips the rest of the way to his.

They kissed until he had to hold on to the edge of the worktable just so he could stop his hands from taking her and hauling her up against him. A noise somewhere cut into his concentration enough that he could recall how Lisa wanted to take things…slowly.

This was going to be tough.

Or maybe for right now, not so tough.

Kevin identified the sound that had been distracting him as the sharp clatter of a wooden yo-yo bouncing against the tile floor.

"What'cha doin'?" Jamie asked.

Kevin stepped back, but kept his attention on Lisa. *Please don't let me see regret for that kiss.*

She smiled at him, then looked past him to Jamie.

"We're being happy, sweetie," Lisa replied.

And those were the best words that Kevin had heard in one helluva long time. If ever.

DINNER WAS WRAPPED UP, the dishes cleared, and all that remained was the original purpose of the meal...the details of the Thanksgiving pageant. Lisa had ducked the topic as long as she could. While Kevin relaxed on the sofa, and Jamie closeted himself in his bedroom to do battle with his yo-yo, she slipped into her room and retrieved the pageant info she'd gathered from Hillside's hummingbirds from her dresser.

"So let me see what I've signed myself up for," Kevin said when she reentered the room.

She settled next to him and handed over the notes. "You really don't have to do this, you know. Jamie would get over it."

Kevin briefly glanced over at her while thumbing through the information. "Careful, or you're going to give me some sort of rejection complex. I told Jamie I'd do it, and I'd never let him down. Besides," he said, waving a page at her, "set construction is right up my alley. I'll call the head dad and volunteer the back of my shop. It's the slow season. We have the room and the supplies to build the trees they need."

And yet another connection was to be forged.

"I feel like we're taking over your life," Lisa said.

He laughed as he set the paperwork on the coffee table. "Hey, I'm a little more multidimensional than the props we'll be building. I still have my job and friends and family, okay?"

It felt distinctly not okay to Lisa. Life had been closing in on her enough without this complication, but she'd have to deal with it. She saw no choice.

"If it gets to be too much, you'll let me know?" she said.

The concerned look he gave her went well beneath her skin, all the way to her heart. "If you promise to do the same in return, absolutely."

She hated feeling like such a prima donna. This wasn't her style. "I know I'm being kind of weird about this, but—"

He gently settled his hand against the side of her face. "Don't…. Don't try to excuse your feelings or discount them, either. This is new territory for both of us, but if we communicate and take it one day at a time, we should all be fine."

Communication. Now there was a concept. She'd had precious little of that in her marriage. Her pregnancy had been a surprise to them both, but she'd been sure that James would adapt to fatherhood. That he'd at least engage, rather than view his son as a new set of chores. How could he not? Jamie might have been unexpected, but he'd been the most beautiful baby, plump and serene. But James had never quite connected, and their marriage had begun to fray. Whether that had been James's fault, hers or both of theirs didn't matter; the end result had been the same. Lisa knew that her communication skills were rusty.

"I'll try to let you know how I'm feeling," she said. "That's the best I can promise."

"Hey, that's the best anyone can," Kevin replied. "Now how about if I take a minute and call this guy?" he asked with a nod to the pageant notes. "Then we can get the focus back where we need it…on us?"

How did he know just the right thing to say? She felt some of her tension recede. Maybe she could do this, after all. Maybe her time for happiness had finally arrived.

"I'd like that…very much," she said.

THE FOLLOWING TWO WEEKS blew by at a crazy pace for Kevin. He had the Alden bid to deal with during the day on top of all his other work, and renovations on his own fixer-upper at night. But most important of all was his time with Lisa and Jamie. So far in the great battle to keep all matters equal, the scale was tipping heavily toward time with Jamie.

Kevin had worked things out so that the Hillside gang got together at his shop Monday and Thursday evenings at six-thirty. First up on the list had been to create the trees for the pageant's forest setting. As it turned out, a couple of the dads were actually pretty handy with the jigsaw, so they were almost able to keep up with the mad painting skills of Jamie and the other kids. It was a toss-up to see whether the tree trunks and branches would wear more paint than the children.

This wild Monday night, the kids had gotten the lion's share. Jamie was one continuous splatter of paint from head to toes. While Kevin was looking forward to being done with the painting and on to gluing autumn-colored paper leaves onto the tree frames, he shuddered to think what the kids might be able to do with glue.

Because he was becoming attuned to what Lisa could deal with and what she couldn't, he had every intention of scrubbing Jamie down in Shortbread Cottage's kitchen as soon as they arrived. The interior of his truck, he'd address later, he thought, giving a wry glance at the smudged, brown handprints Jamie was currently placing on the passenger window.

Kevin parked in front of Lisa's place, then went around to help Jamie out of his car seat.

"Hang on while I get your seat, buddy," he said to the little boy, but Jamie was already cruising up the walk to the café entrance. More handprints to clean for sure, since he was going to beat Kevin to the door.

They were at the sink, and Jamie on his second round of singing "Happy Birthday"—which Kevin totally didn't grasp—when Lisa entered the kitchen.

"Who won tonight, the kids or the trees?" she asked with a nod toward the paint that still marked Jamie's face.

"The kids…again," Kevin replied.

"Think you can have him clean by Wednesday?" she asked, her voice light with laughter.

"It's possible, though not probable."

Especially since out of the corner of his eye, he could see Jamie tiptoeing away, taking advantage of the fact that the grown-ups were all wrapped up in each other. Kevin quickly shut his mind to the other ways he might be wrapped up with Lisa. He was going to take this at the slow pace she desired, even if it killed him. And it just might.

She waved a hand in front of his face. "Hey, are you okay?"

That was open for debate, but he fibbed a little and said he was fine.

"About Wednesday," she said. "It's Inquisition Night."

"Ah. Steeling yourself already?"

"Watch and learn. You're going to need it."

"What do you mean?"

"It seems that my mother's curiosity has been piqued. Your presence has been firmly requested."

"Really? Why?"

Could this be a "meet the parents"? Were they actually going to move past stolen kisses when Jamie wasn't looking?

"I'm guessing it's because Jamie can scarcely get out a sentence without your name in it. In Mom's words, she wants to see who this Kevin is."

Okay, so it was more of a "meet the grandparents." Kevin would take what he could get, especially if it was being offered by Lisa. Better that than feeling as though he was forcing himself on her.

"So what do you say?" she asked. "Ready for a command performance?"

"Sure. What time on Wednesday?"

"Six," she said. "Meet me here and we'll all go together. It will be safer for you that way."

"Do I look like I need a bodyguard?"

She shook her head. "You don't know the half of it, my friend."

Chapter Seven

Lisa loved her mother, yet she had to wonder why it was that a woman who had made a living communicating with others would now pick up a phone only when it suited her? Wednesday morning, she pulled into her mom and dad's driveway. She needed to smooth the path to Kevin's first Inquisition Night, more for her own peace of mind than his. If he could deal with a pack of Hillside kids and dads in his shop on a twice-weekly basis, he had the Zen thing down. Lisa, however, did not.

"This is Grammie's house, not Miss Courtney's," Jamie pointed out from the backseat.

"I know. Mommy just needs to talk to Grammie for a minute. Let's go on in and surprise her."

"'Kay."

Though it was just past seven, Lisa knew that her early rising dad would already be at the office. Her mom's schedule these days, she was a little less certain of.

"Mom?" she called as she closed the front door behind herself and Jamie.

No one answered.

"Let's go check the kitchen," she said to Jamie, who nodded in agreement.

There, she found her mother, dressed for the job she no longer had. Lisa let her gaze drop to floor level. High heels, even. One would think after thirty years in them, sneakers would sound pretty appealing.

Her mother looked up from her laptop computer. "This is a pleasant surprise."

"You're a tough woman to track down," Lisa said. "I've been trying to reach you."

"I had you penciled in for a return call later this morning."

Lisa laughed. "Good to know."

Her mother gave a brisk nod. "But as long as you're here, Jamie, why don't you go on up to your room? There's a little surprise waiting for you."

"Really?" he asked, his voice rising on a note of excitement.

"Would Grammie tease you?"

He shook his head vehemently. "Nuh-uh."

"Then go on," Lisa's mom said.

Jamie needed no more encouragement.

"What was that about?" Lisa asked as she pulled out a chair opposite her mom.

"Nothing. Just a trifle."

Her mom had sounded a little too casual to be believable, but Lisa let the matter rest.

"Kevin is coming to dinner tonight," she said.

"So your voice mail told me," her mother replied. "Did you want to discuss the menu? We're having citrus-honey glazed Cornish game hen and a mix of oven-roasted sweet potatoes and Yukon Golds."

"Cool, just so long as you don't plan to have Kevin on a platter, too. For tonight at least, no deposition tactics, Mom. He's off-limits."

Her mother removed her reading glasses and set them on the table next to her computer. "Well, this sounds personal. Is Kevin more than just Jamie's pageant helper?"

Maybe she should have included herself in the moratorium on deposition tactics.

"We've been…I don't know…hanging out together, for lack of a better term."

"Hanging out, as in dating?"

Lisa sighed. "One meal without Jamie, weeks ago. No official dates since."

"But the meal was a date?"

"As it turned out, yes."

"Really? It's surprising you couldn't have identified that going in. And you wonder why I've been pressing you to get out and about?"

"Good news. You can stop pressing." Of course Lisa knew she'd have better luck in asking the Mississippi to reverse its flow.

"How funny, yet somehow fitting. You're dating Kevin Decker…"

Just then, Jamie burst back into the room.

"Mommy, guess what?"

"There was a pony in your bedroom?"

"No! Better! Grammie got me a race-car bed."

"And you can sleep in it any time you want," her mother said to her son.

"Wanna go see it, Mommy?"

No was not an acceptable response, though it covered the way Lisa was feeling. Jamie didn't need a race-car bed any more than he needed his own toy room. She was surprised her mom hadn't yet evicted the plants and let Jamie move into the conservatory.

"You two go on," her mother said.

Lisa gave her a pointed look. "I'll be back," she said, and she meant it as a warning, not a promise.

Jamie took her by the hand and hauled her upstairs to the room that her parents kept for him.

"Look!"

Though Lisa wasn't a racing fan, she'd peg the bed as a Formula One…low, red, sleek and so expensive that she wanted to march downstairs and shake some sense into her mother.

"I wanna sleep here tonight," Jamie said, dancing in place.

"Not tonight, but soon, honey," Lisa promised.

What child wouldn't want to sleep in this fantasy of

a room? In this latest redo—the last one having been just six months ago—her mother had gone all-out with a race-car theme. In addition to the bed was a checkered flag rug next to it, and a low white bookcase packed with new toy cars. Lisa's gaze narrowed as she took in the framed, autographed photos of drivers, be they NASCAR or Indy or Formula One. She had no doubt that all were authentic, too. Heck, Jeff Gordon's came with a "To Jamie."

Sheer overkill.

"Why don't you stay up here and play?" she said to her son. "I'll come get you in plenty of time to go to Miss Courtney's."

As she returned to the kitchen, Lisa collected her thoughts. She needed to put this in perspective. While careful spending was mandatory for Lisa, it wasn't for her mother. She'd worked hard, earned a lot, and Lisa had little say over how she spent her money. Still, she had to believe her mom hadn't thought this wholesale spoiling of Jamie all the way through.

"Impressive," Lisa said as she entered the kitchen.

"It turned out quite well, didn't it?" her mother asked.

"It's astounding."

Her mother's finely arched brows rose even higher. "Am I sensing some displeasure?"

"The room's great. Really. It's the message it delivers that doesn't do much for me."

"What do you mean?"

"Mom, I know you didn't intend it this way, but let me tell you how it feels to me. It feels as though I can't compete."

"Compete? We're his grandparents, for heaven's sake, Lisa. There is no competition here. We're all one family."

Lisa shook her head. "I'm telling you how it feels. My perception, okay?"

"Which is miles away from reality," her mother replied.

"I think reality is a relative thing."

Her mother sighed. "All right, then, tell me your reality, and I'll tell you mine."

Lisa pulled out a chair and sat. "My reality is that I'm a single mother who works darned hard to keep her son on the right path. I want him to understand that things are nice, but not the be-all and end-all. Even before you redecorated, he had a great room here."

"A room you never let him stay in."

"Not true. We've stayed here."

"Easter was the most recent time. I track it, Lisa," she said, waving a hand at her computer.

It hadn't felt that long ago, but there was no denying her mother's love of spreadsheets and accuracy.

"Of course you do," Lisa replied.

"Don't be mouthy," her mother said. "My reality is this. Now that my life is taking a slower pace, I have more time for my grandson and even for my daughter, believe it or not. But it seems that you don't have any time for me. All I'm trying to do is create an inviting atmosphere. I've been plain about the fact that I'd like to see you both move home, and you've been equally plain about the fact that you'd starve in the streets, first."

"Isn't that overstating it?"

"I'm telling you how it feels. *My* perception," she replied, echoing Lisa's own indisputable words.

"Mommy?" called a tentative little voice from the kitchen's arched entryway.

Lisa turned, and her heart sank at Jamie's furrowed brow. The last thing she wanted was for him to hear any discord. No matter what her personal dispute with her mom, they both loved this little boy.

"Can we go to Miss Courtney's now?" he asked.

She looked back at her mother. "Let's talk later, okay, Mom?"

Her mother, who looked just as shaken as Lisa felt, nodded. They both wanted the best for Jamie, but they'd just shown him their worst.

KEVIN WAS WILLING TO CEDE that this might be a meal of inquisition, but the home that Lisa had grown up in was no dank Spanish *castillo*'s dungeon. He might not have grown up wealthy, but he was thankful that his mom had instilled manners into all the Decker kids. Yes, he'd thought Amanda's palate-cleansing sorbet between courses might have been a little show-offy, but at least he'd known which spoon to select.

Jamie looked pretty jazzed by all of the ice cream,

though. He sat in his "special chair" at the head of the table, just like a little king. Lisa had been seated pretty much at the opposite end of the room from her son. Kevin was beginning to wonder if she hadn't exaggerated family dynamics, as he'd first thought. It could be that Amanda was subconsciously engaging in the age-old battle tactic of divide and conquer. But Kevin had decided long before entering this opulent mahogany dining room that tonight, he would be an observer. A journalist reporting from the front lines...

"So, Kevin, tell me a little bit about yourself," Amanda said.

Or maybe it would be the other way around.

"Mom," Lisa cut in before Kevin could begin to frame a safe answer. "This isn't a job interview, and you know plenty about Kevin already."

"It's okay," Kevin said. "What are you curious about, Amanda?"

"Oh, I don't know, exactly... Your family, perhaps. We saw a lot of Courtney when Lisa was in high school, but I've never met your mother and father."

"They moved to Arizona a few years ago," he said.

"And are you close?"

"We talk at least weekly, so I'd say, yes, we're close."

"You talk weekly? How wonderful! Do you see them often?"

Lisa set down her fork with a rattle that elicited a chuckle from her father. Kevin briefly settled a hand on her knee to let her know that he had this under control.

"I've spent the past few winters down there. The Davenport area gets pretty slow for construction once the first snow falls. I pick up small renovation jobs just to keep myself busy and money coming into the business."

"Have you ever thought of moving down there...living in Arizona full-time to be closer to them?" Amanda asked.

"Not really," he replied. "They have their own lives and their own set of friends."

"True, but I'm sure they'd welcome you. Every parent wants to see more of his or her child."

Lisa rose. "Okay, Mom, that's it. Into the kitchen."

"Sit down, Lisa. I was just making an innocent comment."

"Innocent? That was as calculated as they come," Lisa replied. Kevin was relieved to see that she'd sat, anyway.

Lisa's dad, however, rose and went to the end of the table to see Jamie. "What do you say, champ, that we go into your favorite jungle room?"

"Okay, but I still get cake, don't I?"

Kevin had watched the kid eyeing the German chocolate cake on the buffet the entire meal. Heck, he'd been doing exactly the same thing, too.

Lisa smiled at her son. "Of course you do. Grampy will bring you back here in time."

"Care to come along, Kevin?" Bob asked.

In a heartbeat, but he wanted to be sure Lisa was okay with that, first. He glanced over at her, and she nodded her head.

"Sounds good," he said to Lisa's dad.

"I thought it might. Ladies, we'll be back in ten minutes. I trust by then you'll have hammered out a truce?"

From the look on Lisa's face, Kevin had his doubts. He'd come back later and count the casualties.

THE DINING ROOM MIGHT have cleared, but the red haze around the periphery of Lisa's vision hadn't.

"Well, that was fun," she said to her mother. "I have my doubts that Kevin will come back for a second round of this."

"You underestimate your appeal."

"I was referring to *you*."

"Whatever do you mean?"

"I mean that since you've retired, you're not the mom I always told people you were. The nonmeddling, always supportive, amazing mom. Don't get me wrong, I love you as much as always. I'm just finding it darned tough to be around you."

Her mom took a sip of her wine and leaned back in her chair, her usual ladder-straight posture gone. "Well, that hurt. I don't know what to say, Lisa."

Lisa felt more than a little chagrined. While she knew her mom appreciated straight-talk, maybe that had been more razor-straight.

"I'm sorry," she said. "I don't mean to be harsh, but you've been making me feel cornered, which is also one of my hot buttons. Can you please give me some space in which to be an adult?"

Her mother sat silent, regarding her.

"I've really upset you, haven't I?" she eventually asked.

Lisa nodded. "And kind of freaked me out."

Her mother's laugh sounded too close to tears for Lisa's comfort. "To think that I retired partially to make things up to you. Fine job I've been doing."

"Make *what* up to me?" Lisa asked.

Her mother looked down at her hands. "I…I suppose to make up for not being home so much."

Lisa scrubbed her hands over her face. She felt tense, tired and very sorry she hadn't brought this to a head days—no, weeks—ago.

"I can't change the way you feel, Mom, but I can tell you that from my end of the mother-daughter relationship, I have very few complaints. Oh, there's the slinky black dress you wouldn't let me wear to junior prom—"

"Low cut, verging on tartlike," her mother said.

"Which I understand now," Lisa added. "And I had some quibbles about the curfew you and Dad insisted on, but on the whole, I think I've been lucky to have a mom who not only said but always proved that if you work hard, anything is attainable."

"Well, thank you."

"But now let's fast-forward a little. Whatever you think you lost can't be regained by trying to haul me home when I'm closer to thirty than twenty. I'm a grown woman, with a child of my own. I get that you love Jamie. I do, too. I'd give up my life to protect him."

"And I feel exactly the same way about both you and Jamie."

Lisa nodded. "I know you do. The thing is, I need you to recognize my independence."

"Your independence?" Her mother gave a bemused shake of her head. "Lisa, from the moment you dropped out of college and married James, you became a fully independent woman…and far before you were ready. I think perhaps you need to take a moment to acknowledge your own independence. Your father and I were more than happy to loan you the money to start your business, and we'd be far more than happy to help you out now. Why do you always have to fight us?"

"And why do you always have to try to pull me in so hard?" Lisa demanded in the same angry tone that had come into her mother's voice. She paused, then laughed. "I am my mother's daughter, aren't I?"

"You are," her mom agreed.

They regarded each other from across the Irish linen tablecloth.

"How about if I don't pull so hard and you push a little less?" her mother asked after a measured silence.

"Think it's possible?" Lisa said.

"Of course. If you work hard enough…"

Lisa completed the phrase she'd heard since childhood. "Anything is attainable."

Her mom smiled, and Lisa relaxed a little.

"Okay, so how do we work this out?"

"How about if I drop the idea of you moving home?" her mother offered.

"That would go far."

"But I want to take Jamie now and then, for all of our good. You're his mother, and I will always respect that. I think you sometimes forget, though, that I'm his grammie, and now that I have the time, I want to be a part of his life…and in a more meaningful way than dinners once a week. Do you think that would work for you?"

Lisa thought back to something Kevin had said weeks ago: *Maybe if you let them help more, they wouldn't push so hard…* Smart man, Kevin Decker.

"What do you propose?"

"Let me take Jamie from Courtney's to Hillside Academy. Let your father and me have him overnight now and then. I don't think you've had a single night away from him, and it's time that changed. He's not a baby anymore."

"I know," Lisa said. "There just hasn't been any reason to be apart."

"I can think of one," her mother replied. "The fact that you need a night for yourself. Say, maybe next Monday night? Your father and I have date nights this weekend or I'd offer to do it then."

"You have date nights?" Lisa asked, distracted by the concept.

"Of course," she replied. "At least once weekly.

More, now that I'm not working and can arrange some fun things. I've reserved the honeymoon suite at The Abbey Hotel. It has the most fabulous—"

"Monday would be fine," Lisa quickly replied. Anything to block the flow of too much information. She really preferred not to think about her parents' love life. Among other things, it reminded her of her lack of the same.

"Okay, no more talk of honeymoon suites," her mother said. "But I just have to wonder, what are *you* going to do with that whole night to yourself?"

Chapter Eight

Lisa lurked outside the door of her son's room, where she'd left Kevin sitting on the foot of Jamie's bed, chatting it up about the Thanksgiving pageant and what they would be working on next Monday night. She'd tried to linger for some of the talk, only to be banished by her son because if she heard, it would "mess up the 'prize.'" Heaven forbid she mess up any prizes. As it happened she had a prize of another sort taking front and center in her mind, anyway…exactly as her mother had intended.

A whole night alone, and what was Lisa to do with it?

She plopped down on the sofa and considered her options. A Reese Witherspoon chick flick retrospective held some appeal. So did a good book, a glass or two of wine and all the chocolate she could eat. Those ideas appealed to her need for leisure, if nothing else. But another need kept calling to her, one Kevin had awakened, but they had yet to fully satisfy. She wanted *him*. A full, delicious uninterrupted night with him. At least that was what her body wanted.

Her mind? The word *conflicted* didn't begin to cover that territory. Kevin was being pushed on her, and she and Jamie on him, at a pace that made her very, very uncomfortable. And yet she wanted to urge him into yet another role...lover. She was being unfair to the both of them, but she couldn't stop herself. But maybe she needed to stop overthinking—and just start *doing*—in order to chase off that odd emptiness that still lingered deep inside.

She knew herself well enough to accept that she cared about Kevin. She wouldn't hunger for him like this otherwise. She'd never been one for casual flings or sex without a deeper attraction. The most casual kiss shared with Kevin pushed her imagination ahead to other possibilities. She'd never seen him with so much as his shirt off, but she knew the warm, resilient feel of his skin. She knew the hard responsiveness of his body, and she knew her own need was going to make her crazy if she didn't do something about it.

Once she satisfied that hunger, maybe she could start acting like a sane woman again. Maybe she could focus on business more than she had in the past couple of weeks. She'd been paying a price for her distraction in batches of overbaked shortbread and messed-up orders with her suppliers.

Kevin came down the hallway, then sat close enough to Lisa that she could pick up the spicy scent of his aftershave. Just the smell made her want to move closer, so she did, earning a look of slight surprise followed by a smile as she snuggled in. She'd take her small thrills where she could get them.

"Interesting night," he said.

"Very."

"Nice that you and your mom didn't manage to kill each other."

She laughed. "We've lasted this long, so we'll probably last a few more decades, even if we do scare people in the process. Thanks for your concern, though."

"No problem, but I have to admit that I'm thinking of me, too. If homicide had been involved, I might have missed that German chocolate cake."

She nudged him on the chest. "I know where I rate."

He tipped her face up to meet his eyes. "Seriously, you rate far above German chocolate."

"Definitely good to know."

Now if she only knew how to lead this conversation where it needed to go. She had told Kevin she wanted to take matters slowly, and he had honored her choice. If they were to move ahead, she would have to point-blank let him know that was what she wanted.

"What's up?" he asked. "You're brooding."

"Brooding? No. More mulling."

"Okay, then what are you mulling over?"

All she had to do was say it: *I need for us to make love.*

She drew in a deep breath and tried to form her thoughts.

"I don't know how it happened, but I seem to have agreed to let Jamie have a sleepover at Mom's this coming Monday night," she instead found herself saying in a ditzy-girl voice that made her feel as though she'd been possessed by Malibu Barbie or one of those annoying chicks on MTV's reality shows.

Kevin gave her a what-the-heck? look. "That doesn't sound so bad. He'll have fun, and you can kick back."

"Yes, well…I was thinking maybe you could kick back with me?" she blurted.

"Sure," he said. "I could bring over some movies, or maybe we could go out."

"Out would be good, in a way. This will be my first full night away from Jamie." She'd lost the Barbie tone, but words were still tumbling from her nearly at the speed of sound.

He leaned back a little and looked her square in the eyes. "Ever?"

"Yes, ever."

"Wow. So a nice dinner, maybe?"

She drew in a breath and told him what she *really* needed. Or at least what she thought she really needed. Her excitement seemed to be edging its way toward a case of nerves, but all she could do was push on.

"I was thinking more about a whole night. With you."

Now he was paying attention. "The whole night?"

"Until morning."

"You're sure?" he asked.

His question was casually delivered, but she saw both the focus and the passion in his eyes. She was sure that he'd make love to her with that same intensity, and the thought sent a honey-slow-and-sweet shiver through her. Because she needed to be closer in order to chase away her nerves, she brought her arms up around his neck and kissed him.

"Yes," she said. "All night."

He kissed the spot on her neck—just beneath her ear—that never failed to make her want more.

"I want this to be your choice," he said. "No pressure, okay?"

"Okay," she said, but this didn't feel about choice, and it *did* feel all about pressure. It was as if their steam locomotive of a relationship had barreled on to this station.

Kevin kissed her deeply and hungrily. Lisa tried to focus on just the feeling, but all around her, worries drifted like smoke.

Was she conflicted?

Yes. Crazy conflicted.

Kevin stopped kissing her and sat back on the couch.

"What?" she asked.

"Okay, whatever it is that's been bothering you, tell me, Lisa. If you can't do that, we probably aren't ready to do anything more."

"You could tell that something was bothering me?"

"You're asking if I could tell that you went on a mental vacation in the middle of a kiss?" He shook his head. "Of course I could."

This was new territory. She wasn't accustomed to being around someone so attuned to her. Honestly, it didn't help with the discomfort factor. All the same, he was right. If she couldn't talk to him, how did she expect to make love with him? It was time to leave Malibu Barbie fully behind.

"What I need to know is whether you're with me romantically because you feel some sort of responsibility toward me?"

"Wow. A while back that would have been a fair question, but I didn't expect to hear it now."

"I really need to hear the answer." She knew he wouldn't lie to her, even if the truth hurt.

"Okay. Here goes. After James…um…" he began, then trailed off.

"Died," Lisa offered.

"Yes. Died…"

She placed a hand on his leg in a conciliatory gesture. "This talking thing has to go both ways, you know?"

Kevin nodded. "You're right. I've wanted to bring this up for so long, but now that we're talking about it, I realize I never quite got all the words straight in my head. Anyway…when I first started coming to the bakery every day, I guess you could say a sense of responsibility drove me, but I think it's closer to the mark to say that I cared. That I was worried."

"*Worried?* What is it with people worrying about me?"

"I'm talking then, not now. And was that so strange? You were a young widow with a baby and a relatively new business…not to mention the fact that I'd known you since you and Court started hanging out together in grade school. Yeah, worried."

She frowned. "And so now?"

He shook his head. "I'm not sure who you're selling short, you or me. Either way, let me spell this out for you. Yes, I started coming around out of a sort of guilt. I was James's boss. I was there when the accident happened. I felt like hell. But do you know what? It's been over three years, and I'm still coming around. I'm past the guilt. And I don't look at you as some sort of atonement program. I look at you as a woman...one who I find amazing."

"You've never talked about it," she said quietly.

"What? Finding you amazing?"

She knew he was trying to bring a little lightness to the moment. It wasn't going to help, but her throat felt tight with gratitude that he'd try.

"No," she replied. "About that day. About how James fell. I mean, Scott has talked to me, but you...you never said much of anything."

"You don't remember in the hospital...when I spoke with you?"

She shook her head. "No. I was on adrenaline and autopilot."

"Amazing."

"What?"

"I've been beating myself up over something you don't even recall."

"What do you mean?"

"I tried to say something at the hospital but messed it up so badly that I never knew how to fix it. And so I started visiting you..."

"Not the most auspicious start, and now here we are," she said.

"We are. And there's no changing the past. But you know what? Our future is what we choose to make of it."

And that was something she believed wholeheartedly.

"So, are we okay?" he asked.

She tilted her head and looked at him. He was so many wonderful things: independent, hardworking, kind and darned sexy.

"I think we're better than okay," she replied.

But still the ghosts of worry lingered.

SUNDAY AFTERNOON, Kevin stood in the middle of his semirenovated residence, awaiting Courtney and Scott's arrival. He'd skipped their planned lunch at Malloy's to focus on bigger issues. And he had those, all right.

As if it wouldn't be enough pressure to make love to Lisa for the very first time, it also had to be her first night away from Jamie?

He wanted Monday night to be perfect for Lisa. Unforgettable. And considering the college-frat-gone-downhill state of his home, it might be for that, alone.

The front door creaked open, then closed under protest. Scott and Court entered the room. His sister looked like she wanted to sit down, but thought better of it when she saw the plaster dust that coated the furniture like powered sugar from Lisa's bakery.

"Mom wants to know if you'll fry a turkey for her at

Thanksgiving," Scott said by way of a greeting. "She's afraid Dad's going to burn down the house."

Thanksgiving. Damn. He'd totally forgotten to discuss that with his siblings. Too much on his proverbial platter, he guessed.

"So, you talked to Mom?" he asked Scott.

"Yeah, about a week after you promised you'd call her back and didn't. You messed with her need to plan obnoxiously in advance and you know that's gotten worse since they moved. Apparently, you and I are taking a road trip, bro."

"Wednesday morning is the best I can do," Kevin said. After all, he had a Thanksgiving show to put on the night before that. He looked at Courtney. "How about you?"

"I'm here. Miss Courtney's is up and running the Friday after Thanksgiving."

"And how do you feel about that?" he asked.

"Kind of bummed that Mom and I can't do our nighttime kamikaze mall trip, like last year."

"Scott can go in your place."

Courtney's smile looked a little bloodthirsty to Kevin.

"Mom would run him into the ground. He'd never survive," she replied.

"Nice," said Scott. "And so you've called us together for what?"

"I need your help," Kevin announced.

His baby sister gave a mock-dramatic gasp. "Wait. Say that again. You need *our* help? Did Superbrother maybe trip across a smidge of kryptonite?"

"I'm not Superbrother. Not even close."

"Sure you are," Court said. "Too much so, which is why I'm liking this new, needy side."

Scott laughed.

"I want to have Lisa here tomorrow night," Kevin said, figuring it was past time to redirect the conversation. "Her mom is taking Jamie overnight, and I—"

"Yeah, kryptonite," Scott said, cutting Kevin off. "Very pretty kryptonite. That's romantic and all…" He took a look around. "Did you ever think of maybe going to her place?"

"Not a chance. I think Jamie's the greatest kid on Earth, but tomorrow night should be a Jamie-free zone. No reminders that her son is away from her for the first night, ever."

"Ever?" Courtney asked.

He nodded. "Ever."

His sister's whistle was low and meaningful. "Now that's pressure."

"I had noticed. Which is why I've called us together. I want this place to be perfect, or as close to it as I can get. Scott, I want privacy. I need you gone for the night."

"But where am I supposed to go?"

"I don't know. Stay at Court's," he offered.

"No way," Court said. "I saw what happened when he asked to stay on your couch for a night. You don't own the house or the couch anymore, and he's still with you."

"True," Kevin agreed.

"Hey!" Scott cried. "I'm right here in the room. Stop talking about me in the third person."

"Nothing personal," he and Court said at the same time.

"Yeah. Right," Scott replied. "This arrangement has been pretty convenient for both of us, you know."

"True, again. We've both saved money, and neither of us has needed a dog for companionship. Though Mount Scott, over there, seems to be developing life," Kevin said, pointing at the pile of winter clothes his brother had dumped in the corner…last April.

"Fine. I'll take my clothes, jam 'em in my room, and then go all the way to Illinois to see if Mike has a place for me to crash."

"Yup, all the way across the river works for me. But maybe first you could help me get the rest of the drywall up in the stairway?"

"Like, tonight?"

"That was my game plan."

Scott looked genuinely ticked. "Sure. Why not? Good old Scott is game for anything, right?"

Kevin watched as his brother turned away.

"Scott, this is important. I want the place to look better, if not nice."

Scott turned back and looked at him for a moment. "Okay. But in exchange, you drive all the way to Arizona for the Thanksgiving trip. And we use your truck. I don't want the miles on mine."

"Deal. I drive to Carefree."

He might be hallucinating dancing elephants on the

roadside by the time he finished the trek, but sure. Hanging drywall in a stairway was not a one-man job, and Kevin knew that the stray members of the bat clan that had worked their way into the attic used the open wall as their route to flit around the house. He wanted no spectators to chase out a window tomorrow night.

"Good enough," Scott said, then scooped up an armful of his clothes and trudged from the room.

And now that the basics had at least been addressed, Kevin moved on to the pampering program. Lisa would never do it for herself; her bath truffles sat unused on the ledge above her bath, and he'd yet to see her take an unplanned break.

Kevin looked to Courtney. "What's Lisa's favorite food?"

"Sushi."

"Second favorite?"

His sister grinned. "Sushi."

"I see where this is going. And where do I get sushi?" Which he considered bait not quite fit for the catfish patrolling the depths of the Mississippi.

"There's a place just outside Iowa City. It's really fresh and good. All the Iowa State students go there."

"We have colleges in Davenport. Any chance we have good sushi?"

"Yes, but her favorite is from Cherry Blossom."

"Which is in Iowa City."

"You've got the picture, big brother."

"Okay, so I'm driving to Iowa City tomorrow afternoon." A two-hour round-trip didn't leave him one whole heck of a lot of time to pull this place back from the brink of ruin.

Courtney's eyes widened. "This *does* matter, doesn't it?"

"Let's keep that among the Deckers, okay?"

He didn't want to freak Lisa out. True caring might not fall this early under her step-at-a-time dating program. He was all the way there, and thought that maybe beneath her layers of wariness, she was, too, but why push the point and make her bolt?

"Sure thing," Courtney said. "And, Kevin…?"

"Yeah?"

"Sooner or later, I'm going to tease you about this dating drama."

He wrapped his sister in a hug. "Of course you are. Just let me survive it, first."

He could sense Court's smile if not see it.

"Kryptonite," she said. "I knew it all along."

Chapter Nine

On Monday evening, Lisa pulled up outside the redbrick building that housed Decker Construction. It was a solid, good-looking place, with dark green shutters and perfect landscaping, precisely what she expected from Kevin. After all, he gave every appearance of being a "what you see is what you get" sort of man. She scowled at the perfect building as its front door swung open and a cluster of Jamie's classmates and their dads departed, their work done for the day. She summoned a cheery wave when they noticed her. That small act had taken a lot of effort because on the inside, she remained a weird, edgy mess.

She'd been pushed this far along in her relationship with Kevin—if it could be called a relationship—by circumstances, her son's needs and, now, her libido. Her brain darned well deserved a say, too. And it was telling her to run. She couldn't, of course, not with Jamie inside, and not with Kevin so woven into their family life.

Lisa exited the car and then stopped to exchange brief hellos with Carrie's Dad and the little humming-bird-in-training. Once those last stragglers were gone, she stepped into the building. The small front office was cluttered, yet still managed to seem cheery with its classic black-and-white checkerboard linoleum floor and 1950s desk and wooden desk chairs an interior decorator would probably kill to own.

"Hello?" she called.

"Back here," answered a deep voice from beyond an open doorway.

Lisa wandered through, then stopped and laughed at the miniforest taking up the back of Kevin's shop. It was impressive, maybe even a little overwhelming.

"Hi, Mommy," she heard her son add, but she couldn't yet catch sight of him.

"Should I leave a trail of bread crumbs?" she asked.

Kevin stepped out from behind a majestic oak with a wide trunk and fluttery fall foliage. "It might not be a bad idea." He gave her a sheepish grin. "I think we all got a little carried away with ourselves on this tree-making project."

Lisa laughed in spite of her nerves. "Don't sweat it. Hillside's auditorium is Broadway-size. One semitruck of trees from now, the preschool will have a pageant for the record books."

"So are we ready to get out of here?" he asked. "I can come with you to drop off Jamie or meet you back at my place."

She glanced at Jamie, who was watching them, his face alight with curiosity.

"How about if I catch up with you?" she said in a low voice to Kevin.

She didn't want to have Jamie figure out that Mommy was having a sleepover, too. He seemed to take Kevin as a given in their life. Too many lines between had been blurred already. It was one thing to confuse herself, but another entirely to confuse Jamie.

"Ready for a night in a race-car bed?" she asked her son. "I'll bet it's going to be lots of fun!"

"It's big. You and Kevin can fit, too, Mommy."

She choked back a nervous laugh, and saw that Kevin had had to turn away to mask a grin.

"Thanks, honey," she said. "But this is your special night with Grammie and Grampy."

And she would hope for a special night of her own.

THIRTY MINUTES LATER—at least ten of which had been spent deflecting questions from her mother, who seemed to have selected Kevin-as-son-in-law for her newest campaign—Lisa drove to the home address Kevin had given her. He'd warned her that the house was in the midst of renovations, and more wreck than reclaimed. She felt that way, too.

She was suffering from a self-inflicted case of the crazies. Somehow, she'd spooked herself over an act that was as natural as breathing. And a lot more fun, too. She should accept that she was physically attracted to

Kevin. And she should accept he was attracted to her, too. Maybe even feel a little smug about it.

Years ago she'd had that sort of attention, and years ago she'd last made love. James had been disinclined, to say the least, after Jamie had been born. At first she'd thought it was because she'd put on a few pounds while pregnant. Babies had a way of doing that to a woman's shape.

Once she'd taken the hint, she'd simply shut down her sexuality. Now, after those arid, dormant years, she was bringing it back on line. Natural. Normal. And totally terrifying.

She figured that by now, with all that had been thrown her way in not quite twenty-six years, she should scarcely flinch in the face of more change. Apparently, not true. One question had her as twitchy as could be.

What if she was a failure at lovemaking?

It was possible; she was rustier than her car's dinged-up exterior. And she wasn't without a few emotional and physical dings, either. She had begun to consider Kevin a true friend and a trusted advisor. If they fizzled as lovers, he'd move on. Maybe she wouldn't see him as much, and their current level of closeness would be gone, for sure. She wasn't crazy about the idea of risking what they did have together for something that just might not work.

Lisa slowed to check the addresses on the old homes that sat shoulder to shoulder on the steep road. As she did, another thought occurred.

What if their lovemaking was stellar?

She knew enough of Kevin to realize that he'd want to deepen the bond between them, and that scared the stuffing out of her. But no matter what, she wouldn't have to worry for long.

This morning, when she'd dropped off Jamie at day care, Courtney had brought up the subject of Thanksgiving. She was going to be on her own. Apparently, Kevin and Scott were heading to Arizona the day prior to see their parents. Naturally, Lisa had invited her to her annual Shortbread Cottage Thanks East Davenport extravaganza of a meal. Lisa loved Courtney and could use her help, too.

Courtney had added that their dad was going to lobby hard for Kevin to stay until spring because there was a lot of building going on. From his years coming into Shortbread Cottage, Lisa knew that Kevin tended to spend a stretch of time there in the winter, anyway. Thanksgiving was less than six weeks off. No matter how messed-up things got, she had until spring to recover. That provided some pretty backhanded solace.

Lisa slowed to a crawl. Kevin's truck was parked in the drive of the next house on her left, a white farmhouse-style place in serious need of a paint job and more landscaping than two sad-looking rhododendrons. She pulled in behind the truck, turned off her car and drew the rearview mirror to an angle where she could scrutinize her own paint job…to the extent that a little lip gloss and mascara qualified as paint.

She was as ready as she was going to be. Whatever happened tonight, she had made the decision to be here, and that she would have to view as progress. She grabbed her big purse, which she'd packed with overnight necessities, and exited her car.

The wooden steps to Kevin's front door were new and fresh, unlike the covered porch itself. She did like the cerulean-blue that someone had long ago painted the ceiling, at least where it still clung to the tongue-and-groove wood. Hiding her nervousness behind a smile, Lisa rang the bell.

"Hey," Kevin said when he opened the door. "I'm glad you're here."

"I'm pretty sure I'm glad I'm here, too."

"Just pretty sure?" he asked as he ushered her inside.

She waited until he'd closed the door, then moved in for a kiss. It was warm and welcoming and made her toes tingle just a little. "Okay, very sure."

"Come on into the living room. I've tried to make it livable in honor of your presence."

"So I see," she said. She ran her hand over a square and bulky object that stood about chest-high and had been covered with a sheet. She noted that a few other ghostly objects had been tucked into corners. All he needed were some cobwebs and skeletons and he had the makings of a spook house.

"Getting ready for Halloween?" she asked.

He smiled. "Nothing so exciting. That one's a radial arm saw. I figured it wasn't much to look at."

She tapped another of the room's draped occupants. "A shop vac, right?"

He nodded. "Good for cleaning everything, including Scott when he's passed out on the sofa."

She looked at the plump brown leather couch in question.

"Don't worry. I cleaned it," Kevin said. "Why don't you have a seat?"

She sat on the sofa. Next to her was an antique side table that had been dusted. Its modern chrome lamp had not. Lisa smiled at the eclectic bachelor surroundings. This was so different from her tidy life.

"Speaking of Scott, where is he?" she asked.

"He's over in Moline with Mike. I don't think he'll be back tonight," Kevin said casually.

Too casually.

"You booted him out, didn't you?"

He gave her a broad smile. "You bet I did, and without a moment's guilt. Now, can I get you something to drink? I have water, wine, beer, soda and sake."

"Sake?"

"It goes with our dinner."

"Which is?"

"Sushi."

"You're kidding! I love sushi."

"So I've been told. Hang on… I'll be right back."

Kevin left the room, but soon reappeared with a tray that he set on a low coffee table and then pulled closer to her. Lisa felt decidedly blissed-out at the sight of tuna roll, shrimp, roasted river eel and a few more of her favorites. Sushi was a treat she didn't get often, since it was hardly Jamie-food.

"Somehow I'm guessing you didn't slave in the kitchen over this," she said.

"Not a chance. It's from Cherry Blossom," he said.

Now she knew who the sushi snitch was. She and Court had happened across the place when they—and Jamie—had taken a daylong road trip several months ago. Jamie had slurped his way through a massive bowl of *udon* noodles that she'd cut up for him, while she and Court had gone broke on sushi, which wasn't cheap.

"So you drove an hour, one way, just to get sushi?" she asked Kevin.

"Your favorite sushi," he corrected.

"At least now I know why Courtney was smirking when I picked up Jamie this morning," she said.

"I'm sure it was a supportive smirk," Kevin replied. "A kind and happy smirk. Those are her specialty."

Lisa smiled. "That, they are."

She dipped a piece of tuna roll into a mound of spicy-hot wasabi, then into the small dish of soy sauce, and popped the morsel into her mouth.

"Good?" Kevin asked.

"Heavenly." And so unexpected. Honestly, anything other than the pizza delivery guy would have impressed her.

"I'm glad."

"Aren't you going to sit down and join me?"

"In a second. Be right back…"

Now that she had taken the edge off her sushi hunger, Lisa picked up one of the paper chopstick packets and freed the implements. She managed to swallow—in a hasty boa constrictor-like way—a piece of California roll before Kevin returned with the sake and two small glasses.

"You're okay with me talking to Courtney about what you'd like, aren't you?" he asked as he poured them each a splash of rice wine.

"Yes…I think. Sort of." She drew a breath and collected her thoughts. "Actually, it's probably because I grew up as an only child, but it feels weird to have your whole family in on tonight. I mean, you kicked out Scott and questioned Courtney…"

Lisa watched as he took a sip of sake and winced.

"Must be an acquired taste," he said, putting aside the glass. "I don't know any other way to do it but the way we Deckers do. We're a team."

A pang of yearning sat hollowly in her chest. As much as she insisted on standing on her own, that "team" thing sounded good, too.

"I wanted to make this special for you," Kevin was saying. "I had to ask a few questions of Courtney."

"So, do you at least like sushi?" she asked.

He smiled. "I decided I liked the shrimp once the guy at Cherry Blossom told me it's cooked."

"And the rest of it?"

"Maybe fried up or grilled, or one raw bite after a helluva lot of sake," he said.

She laughed. "I saw the face you made at the sake. You've signed up for your own personal meal from hell, haven't you?"

He gave her a crooked smile. "I can't complain about the company."

"Did you do this just for me?"

"Since you never do anything just to spoil yourself, yes," he said.

She knew she should be touched, but mostly his offerings made her uncomfortable. Kevin had no idea that she'd spent the last year of her marriage listening to James's sad eulogies over the life he'd forsaken *just* for her. The things he'd sacrificed *just* for her. His homeland… His career as a playwright, even though she'd done all she could to encourage him to continue writing. She'd learned that the paybacks for all that manly sacrifice could be a bear to handle.

"So there's nothing here you would have chosen for yourself," she said.

"Ah, but you're forgetting something very important," Kevin said. "I chose *you*."

And with those three words, Lisa's brain finally, blissfully closed up shop for the evening.

KEVIN DIDN'T CONSIDER himself wholly clueless when it came to women. He'd been in committed relationships, and he'd been in relationships that had left him feeling as though *he* should be committed. But at this point in the admittedly young evening, he wondered if he should have skipped the sushi and hired an interpreter of female nuance instead. He understood the words coming from her mouth; the subtext was totally another issue.

Lisa stood and then picked up the sushi tray. "Refrigerator and plastic wrap?"

"Kitchen," he replied. No way was he going to speculate about where this would lead. Instead, he brought her there and covered the sushi for her.

"And now?" he asked.

"I'm assuming you have someplace warm and soft and with sheets used for their original, intended purpose?"

For this he needed no interpreter. "I just might."

Kevin took her by the hand and led her up the newly drywalled stairway, then to his bedroom. Earlier, he'd drawn the blinds and left the bedside lamp on so that the room would be their private space. She entered and, as she had in the living room, wandered and touched... first a picture on the dresser of him with his family, then a thick wool sweater he'd left draped over the arm of his great-grandmother's rocking chair, then the foot of the bed, where an afghan his sister had made for him years ago lay folded.

"Is this what you had in mind?" he asked.

He didn't know which he liked better, her smile or the invitation shining in her eyes.

"Exactly," she said. "Very nice, too. I have to say that's the biggest bed I've ever seen."

Kevin could do without a whole lot of frills in life,

but the one thing he required was a king-size bed. He worked damn hard and liked to sleep well.

"It has lots of room to share," he said.

"I won't take up very much, and it will be right next to you."

"That works for me," he said. "Now, come here."

She hesitated, but then came closer. Not close enough to touch, though.

"It's been a long time for me," she said. "But I guess you've already figured that out."

The thought had crossed his mind. It had been a long time for him, too.

"No rush. It doesn't have to happen tonight," he said. Tough words—ones that fought against every cell in his body—but they needed to be spoken.

Lisa shook her head.

"But I think it does. For me, at least," she said so quickly that one word flowed into the next. "I know I said I wanted to take it slowly, but for the past couple of weeks all I've thought about is what it would be like…what you'd be like."

What *he'd* be like? At that moment the answer was hungrier for her than he'd ever been for a woman in his life.

He watched as she drew a choppy breath, then sent more words reeling his way. "There are all these questions I need to ask…safe sex and all of that…but I've only ever been with James, and all of this is so stupidly awkward for me that—"

He gave her credit for raising all of this, but her nervousness was killing him. He took her hand, brought her up against him, and gave her a kiss that he hoped would remind her who she was with and how much he cared about her.

"I'm healthy," he said. "I've got my doctor's word on it. And I figure you already know this, but I'm not the kind of guy who shares himself with someone new very often. I'll keep you safe. I promise."

And he meant that in more than a safe sex sort of way, though he doubted she'd want to hear that. She was too into making it on her own to recognize that an extended hand wasn't the same thing as one holding her back.

"Thank you," she said and then kissed him so sweetly that he didn't want to let her go. But there was one thing he did want to see let go.

"Could I see your hair down?" he asked.

She didn't speak, but slowly removed the ponytail elastic that held her hair in its workday style and then shook her hair loose.

"Amazing," he said as he winnowed his fingers through it.

Even against his rough palms, it felt like silk. Kevin slipped one hand around to the back of her head and brought her mouth to his. And while he kissed her, his other hand went on a foray for the warm skin right where her top met her jeans.

Lisa pulled back.

"Hang on," she said.

He was, by a thread.

She reached for her top's hem, then pulled the garment up over her head and let it drop to the floor. What he saw next made that thread fray even more: Lisa in a shell-pink scrap of a bra that scarcely cupped her breasts. He reached for her, but she shook her head.

Her gaze locked with his, she toed out of her shoes and then reached for the button at the top of her jeans. His heart slammed loudly, and he was most definitely feeling it in places south, too. She unzipped her jeans and left them at her feet. Her panties matched the bra…lacy, pink and pretty much for decorative effect.

Kevin watched as she turned back the duvet and the top sheet, and then stretched out on the bed. His side of the bed, not that he planned to lodge a complaint. He had spent more than one restless night right there, wondering what it would be like to see her with her hair spread out on his pillows, to touch and taste and give and take pleasure. He'd been a patient man both because it was his nature and because Lisa deserved that and more. This moment was his reward.

"Take off your clothes…slowly. I want to remember this," she said.

And what a reward it was.

Chapter Ten

When had she forgotten about the beauty of a man's body? Lisa couldn't pinpoint the date—didn't want to, anyhow—but she would never forget again. Kevin was beautiful, the sort of lean and muscular man that made her mouth go dry and her pulse hum. She'd known that he was fit. He had to be, given the physical nature of his job. What she had underestimated was her own hunger, how just the sight of him would make her tremble. As he shed the rest of his clothes, she knew she should say something…anything…to ease the intensity of this moment, but she couldn't. All she could do was watch.

"Any other requests?" he asked in a light tone when he was done.

All she could do was shake her head.

"In that case…"

He moved onto the mattress, his weight bringing her closer to him. She resettled on her side and reached out to touch him, resting her palm over his heart. It was drumming as quickly as hers. Feeling bolder, she slid her hand downward to the defined ridges of muscle on his abdomen and traced the thin line of hair that arrowed down to his erection. Beautiful. No doubt about it.

He rolled her onto her back and kissed her deeply. To be touched, to be held, skin against skin. She had forgotten the heavenly heat, the sighs, the whispered words.

"May I?" he asked before unhooking her bra and slipping it away from her body.

"Please?" he asked before sliding her panties down her legs.

And then she was bare to him.

Logically speaking, Lisa knew there was little difference between being naked and wearing the small bits of underwear she'd had on, but now she felt bared…too much so. She wished that she could show the same confidence in her body as Kevin had with her, but James's indifference had left scars. Unlike the silvery stretch marks on the sides of her breasts and low on her belly— what she considered her beloved Jamie marks—these weren't visible. They ran deeply, though. She reached for the sheet, but Kevin stilled her hand.

"You're beautiful."

She turned her face away. "No. Compared to you, I'm out of shape and—"

He put a finger beneath her chin and brought her back so that her eyes had to meet his. "You're beautiful. Inside and out, every day, you are beautiful. Don't hide yourself."

She could feel the start of tears burning in her eyes.

She let her lids slip closed, hoping to fight back the wave of emotion.

"Hey," he said in a soothing voice. "We're new to each other. It's okay. And it's okay to cry, too."

She looked back at him. "I don't want to, but…" She reached one hand up and wiped her eyes. "Damn. I'm sorry. I'm just…"

"Overwhelmed?"

She nodded.

He pulled her closer. "I'll let you in on a secret. So am I. I've wanted this for so long. I've wanted *you*."

"Really?"

"You get the truth from me, always. Besides, you watched me get undressed and you can feel me against you now. It's more than obvious that I find you beautiful and I want you. I told you I'd never lie to you, and my body can't lie. You, Lisa Kincaid, are beautiful."

He slipped down in the bed and placed a kiss just below her navel. "You're beautiful here."

Two slow kisses followed, one for each breast. "And here."

Finally, he kissed her forehead. "And without a doubt, here. You're smart, and brave, and tough. But right now…right here…it's okay to be a little less tough…to let me in. You're safe."

Lisa felt the last measure of reticence melt away. Kevin was a man of integrity, of honor, and that was just as arousing as the feel of his strong body against hers.

"How about here?" she asked, touching a spot on her right collarbone. "Am I beautiful here?"

He laughed, then obliged her with another kiss.

"And here?" She presented the inside of her wrist.

He kissed her there.

"Everywhere," he said, and then proceeded to prove just that.

Time became something without meaning as they learned each other's bodies. Never could she have imagined how well her soft curves would mesh with his hard planes. She was about to reach lower, to touch him more intimately, when his hand closed over hers.

"I'd love it," he said in a thick voice. "But it would be too much right now, okay? In fact…"

He sat up and swung his legs over the side of the bed, then reached out and opened the nightstand drawer. Because she couldn't stand the loss of contact, while he sheathed himself with the condom he'd taken from the drawer, Lisa came to her knees behind him and kissed his neck where it met the broad plane of his back. She knew his low groan was one of pleasure.

He looked over his shoulder at her. "You know that promise I gave of taking things between us slowly?"

She nodded.

"I don't think it's going to be so slow this time."

She settled one hand on each of his shoulders, leaned close and said, "I think we talked about this in lab class. Practice makes perfect."

"Good point," he replied, and she could hear the laughter in his voice.

He reached for the lamp to turn it off, but she stopped him.

"I like it this way," she said. "Let's stay in the light."

He had her on her back so quickly that this time she laughed in surprise. His answering smile was slow and sexy.

"Let's," he said.

And in that moment, she opened herself to him, body and soul. Later, when they both were ready, he entered her slowly. She gasped at the feeling of completion. This wasn't love, she told herself. Love was too big, too scary, too binding. This was passion, hot and perfect, and only for so long as they both wanted it.

Kevin kissed her deeply, then started a smooth rhythm that her body instinctively matched. In time, their dance became deeper, stronger, more assured.

"Beautiful," he said before kissing her, and she held tighter to him…to this moment.

More, he demanded and more she gave. Her skin grew damp and her breath shallow as she reached a precipice she'd not been near in so long.

"You're safe, Lisa," Kevin said. "Come with me, now."

There was no denying the connection, the need, the command. And so she let herself rise with him, fall with him, and spin off into a sort of peace she had never felt before. And later, when she lay with her head pillowed on his chest, she reminded herself that this could not be love.

MORNING ARRIVED WITH the blare of rock music from a radio station not quite tuned in. Lisa came groggily awake in the dim, predawn light and tried to figure out where the heck the music was coming from. She attempted to roll toward the closest edge of the bed, but the covers had been tucked so tightly around her that she was mummy-wrapped.

Kevin entered the room, silhouetted by the light shining in the hallway. He switched off the alarm clock.

"Sorry," he said. "I forgot to turn it off, earlier."

"What time is it?" she asked, combing her fingers through her sleep-mussed hair.

"Early… Six." He sat on the edge of the bed.

"That's not all that bad," she replied. If she were home, she'd be getting up at exactly this time to shower and make breakfast before waking Jamie. Now that her eyes had adjusted, she could see that Kevin had indeed showered. His hair was still sleek and damp, but he was fully dressed.

"It looks as though you've been up for a while," she said.

"Couldn't sleep. Busy mind."

If she were feeling braver, or even slightly more alert, she would have asked what had been keeping his mind busy. Instead she decided to skirt the issue.

"I should probably get up and get ready to pick up Jamie," she said, trying to recall if her purse had ever made it upstairs. Sushi and sake had arrived in the wee hours of the morning, after Kevin and she had made love yet again, but even the evidence of their meal had left the room.

She drew back the covers and moved to the edge of the bed. "My purse…"

"Purse? You mean that giant bag that could house a family of three?"

She smiled. "That would be the one."

"I moved it into the bathroom. I also put out fresh towels for you."

"Thank you," she said as she rose.

She'd thought to slip by him, but he stayed her, then ran his hands up and down her bare arms in a comforting motion.

"I liked having you by me last night," he said. "I liked knowing you were there."

She tilted her head and assessed his expression. Serious. Sincere. And maybe a little sad.

"Even with your busy mind?" she asked.

"Especially."

"Thank you," she said.

She might have told him how she'd awakened in the dark, feeling lost and out of place. But then she'd cuddled closer and relaxed into the steady rise and fall of his chest until sleep had returned. But her feelings were too new, too unsettling to share aloud.

"You're welcome," he replied. "Literally. Any time you want to be here."

She glanced at the clock and thought about the day ahead. Suz was opening Shortbread Cottage, so that was under control. She needed to get Jamie to Courtney's, then return to the bakery and get some fresh scones going. Her life was one tightly timed loop of tasks.

"'Want to' and 'able to' often aren't the same thing," she said.

"I don't know about that. Most of the things I've wanted in life, I've found a way to get."

Kevin was right. And she was evading.

He shook his head, whether impatient with himself or with her, she didn't know. "Go on and get into the shower. I'll have coffee waiting when you're done."

"Thank you," she said for a third time in less than a minute. Maybe she was being a chicken, but at least she was a polite one.

JUST MINUTES BEFORE SEVEN, Kevin pulled up in front of the office. He would have gone in, except Rose and Scott had beaten him there, and he needed prep time before engaging in another round of musical desks with his brother. And so he turned up the tunes in his truck and had a swallow of coffee from his travel mug.

Lisa and he had shared breakfast in the small confines of his kitchen. Although the meal could have been intimate, it hadn't been. Lisa had mentally checked out and moved on with her day as soon as she'd awakened. He couldn't be too critical, though. His restlessness had permitted him to process his thoughts in solitude. To decide how he felt—and why—without an observer. He owed her that much in return.

He'd known that last night was going to be complex. They'd been engaged in a relationship dance long before either of them had recognized it. Sure, he'd gotten there first, but he still had plenty of fodder for introspection.

Was he in love?

Maybe. He had a lot to think about before he knew for sure, though. While he was undeniably a one-woman-at-a-time guy, he'd never been the sort to toss out the word *love*. To him, that was the whole thing...the 'til-death-do-you-part thing. Serious stuff, that.

He knew he was crazy about Lisa. In terms of love-making pyrotechnics, last night had been the best in his life. Not to mention the most exhausting. When he'd awakened at about five, his body had been raring to go again. Finally, though, his brain had taken over and he'd let Lisa sleep. She'd looked so beautiful, so peaceful, and the longer he'd watched her, the more he'd wanted her. And so he'd stepped early into his morning routine. And then in the shower, that word had hit him: *love*. It wasn't going away, but, as with everything else in his life, he'd handle it when the time was right.

With that, Kevin grabbed his coffee and went to wrestle his desk from Scott.

"Good morning," he said to Rose as he entered the office.

"We got an e-mail from the Aldens over in McClellan Heights last night. They'd like to go ahead with us and get a contract written up."

"They understand it's going to be time and materials?"

"They do," Rose affirmed.

Kevin had learned early on that a fixed-price bid when facing an old house with its multiple variables for renovation disaster didn't work. Yes, he lost some business to other contractors. But, unlike those other contractors, he'd never flirted with bankruptcy over a poorly thought-out bid.

"Okay," he said, not fully voicing the relief he felt. Decker Construction wouldn't have a lean winter, after all. "I'll give them a call later in the morning. What's up with him?" he added, with a nod toward Scott, who was facedown, sound asleep on the desk. If he drooled on any paperwork, Kevin was going to kick his butt.

"He was there when I got in. I think he slept here," Rose replied. "Did you two have a spat?"

Jeez, when exactly had he and his brother turned into an old, married couple, having spats? He looked at Scott, whose mouth was slightly open and hair mussed and spiky as though he was trying to single-handedly bring back the grunge rock era. He had to smile.

Love. It came in many forms, and all of them were a little rocky and a lot amazing.

Chapter Eleven

"I had an interesting call last night," Kevin said to Lisa over the counter of Shortbread Cottage, far too many days after he'd last made love to her. Of course, in his book, one day would be far too many.

"Really, who called?" she asked, half paying attention to him and half to her work.

"Your mother."

She nearly dropped the stack of shortbread boxes she'd been carrying.

"Easy there," he counseled as she juggled them onto the back counter.

"Easy?" she asked when she'd swung around in his direction once again. "After telling me that my mother called you? Not possible. Why would my mother call you?"

"Apparently to share something you haven't. It seems you have a birthday coming up."

"It's no big deal," she replied shortly.

He wanted it to be, though. He doubted she'd had a real birthday celebration since before Jamie had been born.

"Maybe I could make a big deal of it?"

She shrugged. "It's just another day."

Suz, who had been eavesdropping from in front of the espresso machine, came over.

"Are you crazy?" she asked her boss. "You've got a hot guy who wants to spoil you, and you're telling him to forget it? No wonder your mother butts into your life."

"Suz," Lisa said firmly. "You, along with my mother, can butt out."

"Hopeless," Suz proclaimed before taking off to the kitchen.

Actually, Kevin was feeling a little hopeful. Suz's drama seemed to have given Lisa some perspective. A smile flirted with the corners of her mouth.

"So come on, birthday girl, are we going to spend the night together on Saturday?" he asked.

She shook her head. "There's one fatal flaw to your plan. My birthday is also Halloween."

"I have a miracle cure. Your mother has offered to take Jamie once we're through trick-or-treating."

She looked at him levelly. "We?"

"Don't worry, I won't dress up or beg." At least not for candy. And he wasn't too sure about the dressing up.

"You're not doing this because my mother put you up to it, are you?"

"What kind of sway could she hold over me?"

"Mom?" She laughed. "It wouldn't surprise me if she had a blackmail dossier on you at this point. You're her new project, you know. She thinks you'd make me a wonderful boyfriend."

He didn't know about the wonderful part, but he tended to think of himself as her boyfriend. Lisa would have to decide that all on her own.

"So are we on for Saturday?" he asked.

She hesitated before answering. "If it's really what you want."

Kevin was beginning to feel at though he'd need his intentions tattooed on his skin before she'd believe him. He pushed aside the slight sting of annoyance and focused on her, though.

"Then we're on. So, birthday girl, want to tell me just how old you'll be?"

She grinned. "Younger than you, my friend."

"Don't worry. I'm not feeling all that old." He could barely believe he was thirty-four. Twenty-four didn't even sound close to the way he'd been feeling since having Lisa in his life. Damn near invincible, however, did.

"Okay, buddy, dinnertime," Lisa called to Jamie, who'd been playing in his room. "Trick-or-treating starts in half an hour. Once you eat, we'll get your face on."

Since he'd been wearing his tiger costume all day and begging to get the matching stripes painted on his face, this news should have sent him running. Instead, Lisa heard nothing in response.

"Jamie?" she called again from the kitchen doorway into the private part of their house.

"I'll go check on him, birthday girl," Kevin offered.

"Thanks," she said, turning her attention back to the chicken roasting in the oven and the broccoli steaming on the range. One last, healthy meal would hit her son's stomach before the deluge of candy and spoiling by Grammie and Grampy began.

And since it was her birthday, Lisa was going to allow herself a little spoiling of her own, too. Later in the evening, after Jamie was with his grandparents, she and Kevin were heading down to Malloy's Pub to meet up with Courtney and Scott. It was to be her first official date as Kevin's girlfriend, or whatever the heck she was. After that, all she wanted for her birthday was a long night in Kevin's arms.

Kevin reappeared in the kitchen. The smile she gave him faded as she took in his serious expression.

"I think you'd better come with me," he said.

"Jamie…?"

He nodded.

Not good.

She followed him back to Jamie's room. Her son lay curled up on top of his bed, knees nearly to chest and eyes closed.

"Hey, sweetie, what is it?" she said as she approached.

"Tummy hurts," he replied in a little voice.

She sat down on the edge of the bed and placed her hand on his forehead.

"He's burning up," she said to Kevin.

"I know. He felt hot to me, too."

She glanced over at him, surprised that he'd thought to do that.

"Hey, I'm not totally clueless," he said. "I had a mom."

She looked back at Jamie, who was still curled up as tight as a little tiger-striped shrimp. There would be no trick-or-treating tonight, not that she thought her son was even in the shape to care.

"Oh, honey, I'm so sorry you don't feel good," she said. "Let's get you in your pajamas." She was going for more than comfort. The tiger costume was one piece, which wouldn't work on a sick little boy.

"No," he said.

She bent close and kissed his forehead. "But we have to."

"No!"

Lisa winced. At least his voice remained in fine form.

"Sorry, but here goes…"

It seemed that passive resistance was a built-in form of protest in a four-year-old. Jamie went limp. Though it wasn't easy, she finally got him out of the costume and into his pj's. And then he started crying in earnest. Between that and the total lack of color in his face, she knew that messy events were about to begin.

"Could you grab the wastebasket from the bathroom?" she softly asked Kevin.

He left, and Jamie started crying harder. Lisa made an executive decision.

"Come on," she said.

Lisa scooped him up, but her maternal instincts had

kicked in moments too late. They didn't even make it from the bedroom before he was sick.

Though her attention was focused on Jamie, she thought she heard Kevin mutter a low "Oh, man." She couldn't blame him. The damage was pretty extensive.

"What can I do to help?" Kevin asked as she carried Jamie into the bathroom.

"Thanks, but nothing," she said. "I've got it handled."

No way would she ask him to address the mess in the bedroom. Being her semiboyfriend didn't put him on cleanup patrol.

"Right," he said.

He'd sounded a little annoyed, but Lisa didn't have time to focus on him.

"Don't worry. We'll get you fixed up," she said to her son as she lowered the lid on the commode and then sat him down. Lisa wiped his face with a warm washcloth and reassured him the best she could that he'd feel better now that his tummy was empty. Jamie wasn't buying in. One sniffle led to another, and then to full-out tears again.

"I'm sorry, Mommy," he wailed between sobs.

"Oh, honey, you couldn't help it. Everything's okay. No one's mad at you or anything."

"But I wanna be a tiger. I don't wanna be si-i-i-ck!"

"Once you're feeling better, we'll have our own special tiger day," she assured him.

"With candy?"

"Sure," she replied, ignoring her own roiling stomach. How could he even *think* of candy at a time like this?

By the time she emerged from the bathroom with Jamie, Kevin had made a nest on the couch, with both Jamie's pillow and favorite blanket.

"Settle him here," he said to Lisa. "Then we'll deal with the rest of it together."

He'd put such emphasis on the last word that she saw no point in arguing. But this felt so strange; she'd never had much help before.

"Look in the bottom of the linen closet outside my bedroom," she said as she got Jamie tucked in. "You'll find a pail, spray carpet cleaner and rags. Just leave them in the bedroom for me."

"Okay."

"Do you want the television on?" she asked Jamie.

Eyes closed, he nodded. Lisa switched on a children's channel. She hoped that the sound would lull him the rest of the way to sleep. She sat there with him for a few minutes, until she was sure he had settled. Then she joined Kevin in the bedroom, where she found him on all fours, rag in hand.

"Hey, you didn't have to start cleaning."

He looked up at her and smiled. "This just didn't seem like a job for birthday girl."

"Let's at least finish this together," she offered.

"How about you go back out there with Jamie, which is really where you want to be, anyway? I'll get this done in no time."

The warmth in his eyes was doing funny things to her knees.

"I have to say this is up there in the top ten of gifts I've ever received. Thank you...very much." And then she went and rejoined her son.

KEVIN DIDN'T KNOW HOW much longer he was going to be able to hold it together. Now that Lisa was gone from the bedroom, at least he could release the grimace that he'd been holding back as much for his sake as hers. A hair-trigger gag reflex wasn't among his most manly attributes, but that's the way it was.

He shook his head as he gave the carpet a second go-over with the stain remover. This wasn't exactly the birthday night he'd envisioned for Lisa. Though he hadn't told her, he'd had Courtney give him a list of people Lisa might want to see on her birthday, then asked them all to come over to Malloy's for a surprise gathering. Now the surprise would be sprung on Courtney, who was going to have to do some quick calling for him.

The gift he'd bought Lisa, he would give her later; but that was just a thing...pretty as it was. What he'd really looked forward to was helping her reconnect with friends who'd fallen to the wayside as her days had grown more filled.

And now he was beginning to grasp how truly hectic and unpredictable a parent's days could be. Parenting took a lot more than a tough gag reflex; it took a level of sacrifice that he might have thought about in passing, but never in depth. He was awed by what Lisa did, and just how well she did it. He'd be kidding himself if he didn't admit that the idea of instant fatherhood made him uncomfortable. He wasn't sure he was prepared. Scrubbing the carpet seemed to be the easy part.

Satisfied that Jamie's room looked and smelled better, Kevin tossed the used rags, stowed the supplies, then washed his hands at the bathroom sink for a good, long time. When he was done, he rejoined Lisa in the living room. A cartoon danced silently across the television screen. Lisa raised her finger to her lips, then pointed at Jamie, who had fallen asleep. Kevin wished the little guy could stay that way until the worst of this had passed, but he knew better.

Lisa then pointed to her bedroom, where they both softly padded. Once they were inside, she closed the door partway, so they could still see Jamie, but not disturb him.

"I'm pretty sure it's just a virus, but I don't like the temperature he's running," she said softly. "I'm going to call my dad."

"Good idea," Kevin said. Having a doctor in the family was a definite plus.

She retrieved the cell phone from her dresser and began dialing. It occurred to Kevin that this was the first time he'd been in her bedroom. Not quite the circumstances he'd wished for, either.

"Hi, Dad," he heard Lisa say. "You're just the person I wanted to talk to. Jamie definitely won't be spending the night. He's running a temperature and vomiting. Have you seen a lot of this at the office?"

Lisa looked over at Kevin and nodded. He never thought he'd be relieved to hear that he'd just exposed himself to some vile bug. Better that, though, than the scary visions of Jamie with appendicitis or god-knew-what-else that had been running through his mind.

"I took his temp just before he fell asleep, and it's still under one hundred," Lisa was saying to her father.

While she answered some more questions, Kevin peeked out at Jamie. He was beginning to move restlessly, his feet pedaling off the blanket that covered him.

Kevin walked to the side of the sofa. Jamie looked up at him and whimpered.

"Going to lose it again, champ?" he asked.

"Uh-huh."

Kevin lifted him, brought him to the bathroom, and rubbed his back while he was once again sick. When Jamie was done, he wiped his face, filled the cup that Lisa had left by the sink, and told Jamie to swish and spit…which he did with great gusto. And when all was done, Kevin gave himself a mental pat on the back for not being the next one to hang over the toilet.

He picked up the little boy, amazed at how tiny Jamie felt in his arms. How vulnerable…

"Everything okay?" Lisa asked from the doorway.

Kevin smiled. "Relatively speaking."

"Bed or sofa?" she asked Jamie.

"Bed." He hugged tighter to Kevin. "With my truck."

Kevin felt honored. Rattled, out of his element and a little queasy…but so damn honored that his throat ached.

CURLED UP ON THE COUCH next to Kevin, Lisa glanced at her watch. Twelve-fifteen in the morning, and she was no longer a birthday girl. She was fine with that, since it also meant that Jamie had slept for over two hours now, with no more need to empty his poor stomach.

She tipped up her head to see if Kevin was still awake, or if he'd had enough of the movie she'd stuck in, and was napping. His eyes were closed and his breathing regular. Sleeping, probably. She snuggled closer, taking the comfort she knew he'd freely give if he were awake.

Tonight had been pretty messy. Without him, it would have been downright awful. Kevin had even gone to the drugstore to pick up the fluid replacement drink her dad had suggested, along with a bottle of her favorite green tea.

"We have to keep the mom going, too," he'd said.

She thought back to the few times Jamie had had health issues as an infant. James had been beyond useless; he'd been an outright impediment. It had been almost as though he'd resented the attention being taken from him. Lisa knew that wasn't a kind thought to have, and probably one that arose more from her resentment than his actual behavior. All the same, the enduring image of her marriage would be James with his back to the two of them.

When Jamie had been tiny and had needed feeding in the middle of the night, she'd quickly learned that it was better to get her son, herself, then nurse and change him, than it was to ask for help. Those times she just couldn't find the energy to roll from bed again and had awakened James, he'd been hostile and nasty. When she'd confronted him in the morning, he had always claimed no memory.

Tonight, Kevin had gone so far above and beyond what she'd expected that she felt nearly suspicious…and a tad guilty for feeling that way, too. Could he truly be this nice? She wanted to believe in him, but after the rocky road she'd traveled with James, she was inclined toward the theory of "If it seems too good to be true, it probably is."

She looked up at Kevin again, and smiled at the way his dark lashes were fanned against his cheeks. Unable to help herself, she sat up and placed a kiss along his jawline, where dark stubble had begun to grow. His eyes came open, and he smiled when he saw her.

"Hey," she said, smiling back.

"Jamie?"

"He's sleeping fine," she said.

"Good," he murmured. "What is it, like ten now?"

"No…. Midnight."

He sat up straighter. "You're kidding."

"Nope."

"We missed your birthday," he said.

"It was one I'd be willing to miss again," she replied.

"No way." He moved her off him, then rose. "Why don't you check on Jamie again, while I get a few things together?"

"What sort of things?"

"You'll see," he said before disappearing into the kitchen.

"All-righty, then," Lisa said to herself.

She stood and tiptoed to Jamie's room. Although his skin didn't hold its usual healthy glow, color was beginning to return already. He slept deeply...peacefully. Lisa wouldn't be surprised if he didn't wake until dawn. She watched him for a few minutes, then silently left the room. As she exited, she caught Kevin leaving her bedroom with the jar candle that usually sat on her dresser.

"What are you doing?" she asked.

"Wait and see."

He disappeared into the bathroom for a moment, came back out, and quickly closed the door. She watched as he took the two taper candles she had sitting on her antique parlor table in the far corner of the living room. When he headed back toward the bathroom, she fell in step close behind him. He stopped dead in his tracks, and she bumped up against him.

"Go sit. No peeking. You'll know soon enough," he said.

"But I want to know now." All the same, she went to the couch and sat.

He gave her a grin before opening the bathroom door and disappearing. In front of her, the movie on the television rambled on. She tried to pick up on the action just to distract herself, but it was a lost cause. What seemed like forever later, Kevin came back into the room and beckoned her down the hallway to the bathroom. The sound of water running tipped her off to a waiting bath. Sweet, really, and she appreciated it.

But then she stepped into the bathroom. It was hardly the same functional yet dull place she'd comforted Jamie in. Where before the old black-and-white hexagonal tile had been relieved only by a small white bathmat—actually slightly grayed with age—there now sat a thick rug in exactly the same shade of periwinkle that she'd painted one wall in her living room. Fat new towels of a deeper hue hung over the towel rack. On the hook by the bathtub hung a new ivory-colored terry cloth robe, so luxe-looking that it would have been at home in a five-star spa. Lit candles lined the far edge of the tub, and a champagne flute awaited her.

"Happy birthday," he said.

"Well, thank you."

"I was going to do this for you when we got home from Malloy's. Of course, at that point, the game plan had been two glasses of champagne and me in the tub with you," he added, then gave her a rueful grin.

"Kevin, it's wonderful."

"Come here," he said, taking her by the wrist and gently drawing her closer. "Relax and let me take care of you."

She wouldn't fight this pampering. She was so bone-tired that just this once, she would put herself into his hands…literally. She watched as with great care, he unbuttoned her shirt and slipped it from her. A sigh of utter contentment escaped as he took a moment to kiss the spot where her pulse danced at the base of her throat.

When he knelt to slip her feet from her shoes, Lisa wanted to cry, both in thanks for his tenderness and because she wasn't so certain she deserved it.

And when he'd removed all of her clothes, he drew her into his arms and held her. The embrace was far from platonic, but she could feel his restraint. After a moment, and one kiss to the top of her head, he let her go, then reached for the box of bath truffles he'd given her weeks ago.

He held it out. "You'd better pick one, quick, before the tub's too full."

She opened the box and gasped. On top of the truffles sat a delicate gold-and-diamond necklace.

"Kevin—"

He shook his head. "Don't tell me that I shouldn't have because you don't get a vote on that one. You do get to decide if you want to be the gracious woman I know you are and accept it, though."

She lifted the necklace from the box and held it aloft, so that its adornment sparkled in front of her eyes. It reminded her of a shooting star, with one larger diamond, behind which trailed smaller ones in a graceful arc.

"It's beautiful," she said. "Thank you. I don't know what to say…"

He reached into the box of bath truffles and randomly tossed one into the tub.

"Exactly that," he replied. "You're welcome."

She set the truffle box on the sink's edge, and he went and turned off the tub's taps.

Lisa opened the clasp to the necklace and tried to put it on. Whether it was her weariness or the mix of emotions that coursed through her, she couldn't work the tiny fitting.

Frustrated, she said, "Would you help me?"

Kevin smiled. "All you ever have to do is ask."

He took her by the waist and gently urged her to turn so that her back was to him. She thought that he'd immediately take the necklace from her, but he lingered, exploring the curve from her waist to hip. Lisa sighed again. It felt heavenly to be touched.

His large hands closed over her smaller ones. He took over the necklace, getting it secured after only a moment. But then his hands drifted downward, over her ribs. She jumped a little.

"Ticklish?" he asked.

"Not usually, but tonight, I guess I am," she said.

"Relax," he commanded and then began kneading her shoulders.

How could a woman *not* relax, when receiving this kind of attention? Slowly, the night's tension receded until all that remained was sheer pleasure. Lisa closed her eyes as he trailed a line of kisses across her shoulders. When he drew her back until her nude body rested against his clothed one, she didn't object.

He touched the necklace, where it lay at the tops of her breasts. "I wanted you to have something to remind you of me."

"As though I'd forget." He was a part of her days, her

thoughts…and although she'd been trying to fight it, her heart, too.

Kevin kissed her neck and brought his hands around to caress her breasts. Her breathing picked up as a delicious sort of excitement curled through her. He knew just how to send her over the edge into passion. But she had her son in the other room, and while he was resting now, she needed to be there for him.

She leaned her head against the strong expanse of Kevin's chest and worked up the willpower to say what had to be said. "We can't…"

"You're right," he replied in a husky voice that sent another thrill through her. "We can't, but *you* can. Consider it part of my gift to you, then you take your bath, and I'll keep watch around here."

She hesitated.

One hand moved lower on her body. "Let me give this to you, Lisa."

"But…"

"It won't take long," he said.

She smiled at the pretty darned accurate assumption. "Braggart."

Once, then again, he brushed his fingers intimately…teasingly…against her. She leaned into him, in capitulation to the pleasure he would bring.

"It's noble of you to sacrifice yourself this way," she said.

His chuckle vibrated through her. "Only for you, sweetheart. Only for you…."

Chapter Twelve

A sunny and cool November lunchtime merely three days later, Kevin watched as Jamie bounded to the swing set at Lindsay Park. The little guy was the portrait of health and excess energy. If Kevin hadn't seen him so sick on Halloween, he wouldn't have believed it.

"If Jamie were a dog, he'd be a golden retriever puppy," he said to Lisa, who laughed.

"How about you? What would you be?" she asked.

He watched Jamie detour for the sheer joy of running in a zigzag pattern. As the years had passed, Kevin had found less and less desire to take the circuitous route.

"An old hound," he said.

"Yearning for the resilience of youth?" she teased.

He swung her in his arms for a quick kiss. "I can think of a few things I'm yearning for more than that."

"Me, too," she murmured.

They hadn't had any alone time, excepting those few minutes on her birthday. While he wouldn't trade his

Thanksgiving project time with Jamie, or a picnic lunch like this one, he wanted more. A lot more.

Last night, he'd called Pop and shot the breeze for a while, then gradually brought the conversation around to Jamie and his horrible Halloween. Kevin had asked his dad how he'd known what to do when Kevin had been little, and his dad had laughed as though he'd told the best joke ever.

"Know? You were our first...our test case. When you were little, your mom and I didn't have idea number one of what we were doing. If it wasn't in *Dr. Spock* or if we couldn't reach your grandparents, we just did our best. Seems to have worked, too, for the most part," his dad had said.

It was then that Kevin realized he was trying to treat life as though it came with blueprints, like one of his construction projects. Even when building, he knew better than to believe that everything was as drawn. Sometimes you just had to wing it.

"Come push me, Kevin," Jamie called excitedly from his seat on a swing.

Kevin looked to Lisa for an okay.

She smiled. "You might as well go on ahead. I'm yesterday's news since you came along."

"I could leave," he teasingly offered.

She planted her hands on his back and marched him over to her son. "Not a chance. You're far too useful."

He'd take *useful* until a better adjective came along. He'd dated enough women in his life to know that Lisa was perfect for him. Jamie, too. Sure, the instant dad thing rattled him some, but life was about challenge and change, and he was ready for both.

"Okay, ready?" he asked Jamie, who gripped the swing's chains tightly and affirmed that he was.

Kevin made a great show of pretending that he was going to send him rocketing to the sky, but then gave him a nice, safe release for a kid his size. Jamie crowed his approval. Kevin stood back and watched as Lisa coached him how to pump his legs and go higher.

"Did I tell you that I got a big, new project not too long ago?" Kevin asked Lisa, while keeping one eye on Jamie.

"No, really? Where?" she asked, her gaze also pinned on her son.

"Do you know where Fairview is?"

She nodded. "That huge place that looks like an English countryside mansion overlooking the river? Sure."

"The owners want to bring it back to its glory."

"All of it? Doesn't it have a ballroom wing and a pub room and bowling alley in the basement?"

"I haven't seen the basement yet, but that's what I've been told."

"Very cool."

"Yeah. It's great news. This is the sort of project that will land us in the glossy magazines. Our reputation is finally getting out there."

"Wonderful," she said. "When do you start?"

"We'll start some of the smaller rooms in the next few weeks, but probably not in earnest until spring."

"That sounds like it works with your usual winter in Arizona plans."

"Actually, I'm thinking of not going this year," he said, almost surprised to hear the words come out. Until that moment, it had been more of an under-the-radar sort of thought than an actual plan. But now that he'd said it, the idea made sense. He'd rather be here.

She turned to look at him. "Why? I thought you loved going there."

He grinned. "Yeah, but maybe I love it even more when I'm useful to you."

Doomed. Lisa was flat-out doomed. Kevin loved going to Arizona in the winter. He'd told her that countless times since they'd been together, and she'd heard it from Courtney even before that. And now he was making noises about staying here.

Under no circumstances was she taking that relationship route again. First came "anything for you," then came "look what you made me do," and finally, stone-cold silence. Thank you, but no. If she'd learned anything from her marriage, it was that she'd never watch another man change for her…ever again.

"This isn't making any sense," she said to Kevin. "First you loved Arizona and now you don't want to go?"

"I just told you that we've got a busy winter lined up."

"Not exactly. You said you were starting the bigger part of the project in the spring."

"The Aldens aren't our only clients," he said. "We have a lot of smaller projects, too. It makes better sense for me to be here than in Arizona. I'm the owner of Decker Construction. I'm responsible for scheduling and for keeping things flowing. I can't leave Scott to twist in the wind."

"That wasn't an issue last winter. You were gone for months." And while she had missed seeing him come in for his morning coffee, she suspected that this year the lonely ache would be as brutal as the winter wind. But she'd rather bear that than feel as though she'd trapped another man.

He frowned. "Hey, what's going on here? Yes, it's a Wednesday, but Inquisition Night doesn't officially start for another six hours. And at this point, I'd much rather be questioned by your mother."

She drew a deep breath and tried to quell the panic.

"Mommy, push me!" Jamie cried from his perch on the swing.

Automatically, Lisa stepped forward and gave her son a little nudge.

"Harder!"

She put a little more force into it this time.

"I wanna fly!"

She looked over at Kevin, who was scowling across the river to the opposite shore, as if the entire state of Illinois had done something to offend him.

Frustrating man! When, exactly, had he forgotten that he wanted to fly, too?

THOUGH LESS THAN A WEEK had passed since Kevin, Lisa and Jamie had last visited the park, November cool had turned to November downright frosty, and Kevin wasn't referring to the weather.

He sat with Scott and Courtney at their usual table at Malloy's, waiting for Lisa to join them. He'd already ordered a drink, shot the breeze with Conal, talked business with his brother, and still Lisa hadn't arrived. He checked his watch.

"It's a quarter after," he announced to no one in particular. "Lisa's never late."

"Think she dumped you?" Scott asked.

"Think you can back off?" Kevin fired back.

"Hey, sorry. I was just kidding. Not to fear. I've had dates show up two hours late."

"And you waited?" Courtney snorted. "Sucker."

"Watch it. It's not as though you're tearing up the dating scene," Scott pointed out to his sister. "At least I get out and try."

Kevin zoned out as his siblings bickered. Normally, Scott's teasing would have rolled right off, but something had changed in the past week. For a day or so, Kevin had just figured that Lisa was extra-busy. She'd started to work on planning her annual Thanksgiving meal for those among her customers who didn't have traditional family nearby to dine with. Her mom was pitching in, too, which was a definite step forward in mother-daughter relations.

But in exchange for that step forward with her

mother, Lisa had taken a step back with him. Nothing he said or did brought a sparkle to her eyes or affected her too deeply. To Kevin it seemed that she'd somehow encased her emotions in a hard crystal shell, and he didn't know how to get through to her.

He had done the emotional math and realized that only one thing had changed since she'd shut herself away; he had mentioned that he was thinking about an Iowa winter. Maybe blurting that out had been a tactical error on his part, but he preferred to think of them as lovers, not military leaders on opposite sides of a battle.

He looked at his watch again.

"Three minutes later than the last time you looked," Courtney said. Which meant, of course, she had looked at her watch, too. His tension must have been pretty obvious because she added, "Relax before you sprain something, okay?"

Scott laughed, and even Kevin had to smile at his sister's mouthiness. So much for having his siblings in awe of him.

"She had to drop Jamie at her mom and dad's, right?" Courtney asked.

"Yes."

"She's a grand total of eighteen minutes late, which is not unthinkable when you have a four-year-old to wrangle."

It wasn't the number of minutes so much as the overall sense that she was about to disappear on him. Maybe it was time to confide in his siblings. Beneath all that mock sparring, he knew they cared. And maybe he was being paranoid, anyway. Maybe Lisa was fine, and he just didn't know her as arrogantly well as he thought he did.

"Court," he said, "have you noticed anything different about Lisa?"

She shook her head. "Not really. She hasn't had the time to stay and talk when she picks up Jamie, and she's—"

"—coming to the table right now," Scott interjected.

"Let's talk later, okay?" Court suggested, her concern for Kevin softening her eyes.

Being able to pick up on that made him feel even grimmer. He knew emotion when he saw it, and could identify the lack of it, too. Kevin said okay to Courtney, then rose to greet Lisa.

"Sorry I'm late. I got a little wrapped up with Mom," she said.

"No problem," he replied as he leaned in to catch a quick kiss.

But as he did, she withdrew. It wasn't as though she turned her face, but she pulled back just enough that the kiss became a marginal brush of one mouth against the other. He gave her a "what's up?" look and got a wide-eyed, innocent "who, me?" expression in return.

She was drifting off. He could feel it in every molecule of his body, and it was really grinding at him that she wouldn't just admit it. Instinct urged him to confront her, but common sense told him to wait.

Not here and not now. But soon. Damn soon.

INQUISITION WEDNESDAY arrived, though the day's sharp tag had lost much of its meaning for Lisa since she and her mom had made peace. Now the talk was of the upcoming Thanksgiving pageant. Her mom and dad were going to be there, of course, but Courtney and Suz were going to attend, too. The more, the merrier, as far as Lisa was concerned. Jamie would enjoy being a celebrity, and she would feel less as though they stood out as a nonstandard Hillside Academy family unit.

Today after school, Kevin and a group of dads had moved all the pieces they'd built for the set to the auditorium. Jamie had wanted to go along, too, but Lisa had asked her mom to bring him to her house. Lisa looked at it as a weaning process; Jamie needed to understand that Kevin really wasn't family. It was a tough process, but inevitable. But because she knew her family expected it—and because she wanted to at least be in his company before she sent him on his way to warmer places, and probably warmer women—she'd brought him along for dinner.

As they walked the steps to her parents' front door, she took a moment to fix in her mind the image of Jamie gripping his hand, and Kevin smiling down at her son. It looked so classically perfect, but she knew how deceiving appearances could be.

Once inside, they found her mom and dad in the library, enjoying glasses of wine and listening to opera. Dad sat in his favorite leather armchair, at a right angle to the sofa where her mom sat watching the flames flicker and dance in the fireplace.

"Is the lady hurt?" Jamie asked about the soprano who'd just hit and held a tragically high note.

"No, she's fine, sweetie," Lisa assured her son while trying not to laugh.

Jamie clapped his hands over his ears.

"Gonna go to the jungle room," he announced, then turned heel and marched out.

Laughing, Lisa's mom rose and turned down the stereo system.

"I suppose it will take some time for Jamie to develop his ear," she said.

Kevin chuckled. "Some of us are still working on it well into our thirties."

"I take it opera wasn't part of your family's listening fare?" her dad asked Kevin.

"Mom likes Broadway musicals, Dad's a country music guy, and all of us kids are rock-and-rollers," Kevin replied.

"Amanda's the opera fan," Lisa's father confessed. "I just listen along to humor her."

But down that road lay ruin, Lisa thought. She glanced at her mother, but Mom looked more lovingly amused than anything. She switched off the stereo altogether, then offered Lisa and Kevin refreshments, as dinner was going to be a few minutes.

Kevin sat in the second leather chair that flanked the

right side of the sofa, and Lisa chose the end of the sofa opposite her mom. She smiled when she realized that as couples, they were mirroring each other. But once again, this was all a surface illusion. She wished that she and Kevin had that common bond that had carried her parents over the years, though she knew better. Her parents were so very lucky.

After the talk turned away from music, her mom brought up Thanksgiving dinner.

"I've contacted the rental company for tables and folding chairs," she said. "While the café setup is lovely for what you normally do, it won't work for a group like this." She looked at Kevin. "Do you think you could help set up the night before?"

"Sure," Kevin said at the exact same moment that Lisa was saying, "He'll be gone."

They looked at each other, and Kevin frowned.

"Pardon me?" Lisa's mom asked. "I think I just received mixed messages."

"Mom, Suz and I can get the tables set up. Kevin has to leave for Arizona on Wednesday morning. He's spending the winter with his parents there." And she dared him to say anything different, too.

Kevin placed his beer glass on the shiny marble coaster that her mom had set on the end table for him. The sharp clattering sound made Lisa jump.

"Amanda, how much time do we have before dinner?" he asked.

"Is something wrong?" her mother asked in response.

This time, Lisa said no as Kevin gave the opposite opinion.

Her mom shook her head. "It sounds to me as though dinner needs to wait. Take as much time as you need."

Kevin rose. "Thank you. We should be just a few minutes."

Lisa felt a little like the kid about to be taken to the principal's office.

"We can do this later, okay?" she asked, actually hoping to avoid it right to the bitter end.

"Now," he said, holding out his hand.

Automatically, she took it, and he helped her to her feet.

"Lisa and I are going to step outside," he said to her parents. "I think some fresh air will do us both good."

Chapter Thirteen

"That was a little dramatic, don't you think?" Lisa asked as Kevin took her jacket off a hook on the antique high-backed bench in the front hallway and handed it to her. Nerves had pushed their way straight into anger. She hated confrontation…didn't know how to handle it.

"Dramatic would have been arguing in front of your parents. This," he said while ushering her out the front door, "is diplomatic."

She paused to zip her jacket, and waited while he did the same. Though it wasn't yet six, the sun was well down in the sky, casting long shadows from the maple trees, which were now bare of leaves. Maybe it wasn't quite bleak midwinter, but it felt that way in her soul. She walked down the steps and just off the sidewalk to stand on the lawn.

"Let's go around to the backyard," Kevin said.

Lisa shook her head. "Jamie will see us from the conservatory windows."

"Right. Okay, then, I guess this is the spot."

186 The Littlest Matchmaker

"It doesn't have to be. We don't need to do this. You could just go on with your plans, and I'll be waiting when you come back in the spring."

She hated the way she'd just sounded…panicky.

"Why are you doing this?" Kevin asked.

"Doing what?"

"Come on, Lisa. This is *me*," he said, briefly placing the flat of one hand on his chest. "You know I feel it. You're closing yourself away."

"No, I'm not." She preferred to think of it as preserving the status quo.

"Bull. What's up with telling your parents I'm going away for the winter? I'm not, and I'd think you'd be okay with that. More than okay, actually. I'd think that you'd want us to have the time together."

"What I want is for you to go on with your plans. You go to Arizona every winter, and that's where you should be."

"What about us?" he asked flatly.

She said the first words that came to mind. "We were a product of outside pressures…me being alone, Jamie needing some help…all that stuff. On our own, we don't mesh."

He shook his head as though clearing a discordant noise from his head. "We don't mesh? You're joking, right?"

He'd started this, but she needed to get through it in order to feel strong again.

"No, I'm not joking." But she was feeling ill with stress. "You know, I like to think of myself as a pretty perceptive guy, but it took me a while to catch on to you. Now I think I get the full picture."

"What does that mean?" she asked.

"It means that when I look at you—*really* see you— I see someone who's beautiful, kind, talented and probably the love of my damn life."

Her heart beat faster, but excitement wasn't driving the rhythm. Fear was. "Did you just say that you love me?"

"If you haven't figured that out by now, we have a lot more to work on than I thought. Of course I love you. I have for years."

She shook her head and took a step backward. "But it will never work. It can't."

"Not unless you work with me, it won't. You need to see me for who I am, just as I see you. You need to let go of whatever happened in that marriage of yours."

"What…what could you possibly know of my marriage?"

She had worked so hard to keep the truth at home, where no one, not even her parents, could know how wrong things had been. All she'd had left was her pride, and it looked as though that had been an illusion, too.

"Come on, Lisa. James worked for me. I saw what he was like. He was drowning in bitterness."

"He was Jamie's father. Don't talk poorly of him."

He took her by the arms. "This is *us*. I told you I'd always give you the truth. That's not going to change now, even if you don't like what I'm saying."

"But he was Jamie's father," she repeated, hanging on the one bright spot she'd taken from that part of her life.

"Of course he was. And I'd never talk him down in front of Jamie. Come on, you have to know me well enough to see that."

The hurt she'd been holding back, the anger, all of the insecurities she'd carefully cobbled over…all of it came spilling out. She wrenched free of Kevin's grasp.

"What do I know? Who am I to figure this stuff out? Oh, I know how you seem on the surface…all kind and wonderful…but even you have to have your breaking point. I refuse to love another man who will have to change himself for me. You said you wanted to go to Arizona for the winter, so go!"

"Lisa, what are you talking about?"

"I know what happens if you don't go. If not six months from now, then a year from now, you'll start resenting me. It's inevitable. And then we'll start arguing, and you'll tell me that I ruined your life. You'll tell me that I don't know how to love, that I'm incapable of it. And then, God forbid, if anything happens to you like it did to James, I'll spend the rest of my life wondering whether it was an accident or by design."

Had she said that aloud? It was horrible enough to even think it. So horrible that she'd never allowed herself to do more than skitter past that particular demon on dark and sleepless nights.

Kevin shook his head. "You think he… You think it wasn't an accident?"

"I don't know. I don't want to talk about it. Not now. Not ever."

He took a step toward her, but she held out her hand, staying him. "Don't."

She watched as Kevin drew a deep breath, then slowly let it go. "Well, if he did, that was the cruelest exit, ever. And you think that I'd do something like that?"

Did she, really? She was too mired in emotion to think clearly. "How do I know? How do I know *anything?*"

"Look at me," he said in a calm tone. "Do I look like a selfish, spoiled bastard? I love you, Lisa. I'd never intentionally hurt you. If you can't see the kind of man I am—one about as far removed from James Kincaid as you can get—it's going to be a huge loss. Not just for me, but for us as a couple, and for Jamie, too."

She stood silent…scared. She wanted to agree with him, but the price was too high. She would not risk ruining another man's life.

Kevin jammed his hands back into his pockets. "So that's it? You have nothing to say?"

She looked at the dead brown sod beneath her feet.

"Maybe you're right. Maybe we don't mesh," he said. He looked down the driveway, to where her car was parked. "Look, I think I'm going to walk home. Tell your parents I'm sorry I couldn't stay for dinner. And tell Jamie… Just tell Jamie that I'm sorry."

But not nearly as sorry as she was.

"I'VE HIRED PAUL NAUGHTON to do the fine carpentry," Kevin said to Scott on Friday as they stood in the office going over the renovation plans for the Aldens' home. Two days had passed since he'd walked away from Lisa. They had been the longest two days of his life.

This coming Tuesday, Kevin was going to drive Scott to Carefree for Thanksgiving. The Sunday after, Scott was going to fly home. Kevin planned to hit the ground running in Arizona and find so much work that he'd have no time to brood. The irony of brooding in Carefree didn't escape him, after all.

But for now he needed to dump as much information as possible with his brother. Rose knew how to keep the office going, but she'd never been involved in estimating or bidding, other than prettying up the finished product.

"Paul's more per hour, but the job will be done right and faster than with the other bidders," Kevin said to his brother.

"Makes sense," Scott replied.

"You're sure you're going to be okay to handle this while I'm gone? Four months is a helluva long time." Not long enough to get over Lisa, but it would have to do.

Scott hitched a thumb toward the wall. "That degree in business and construction management might give you a hint."

"Schoolwork isn't the same as doing it," Kevin pointed out.

Scott smacked down the notebook he'd been using. "It's as damn close as you've let me come. I've been a full-time part of this business for six years and I'm lucky if you let me find my way to the office by myself. I don't want to throw around threats because I'm here for better or worse, but I'm getting sick of the worse, you know? I don't know why, but for some reason I'm fixed in your mind at age seventeen."

"That's stupid," Kevin said.

"Yeah, it is."

"No, I mean that I don't think of you as seventeen." At least, he didn't think he did.

"Then stop treating me that way. I'm a Decker and I deserve to be more than your hired hand. While you're down there sulking at Mom and Dad's, you might spend some time thinking about that, too."

Rose stood and applauded. "It's about time, Scott Decker. *Now* you've earned that piece of paper on the wall."

Kevin looked at his brother and shook his head. "So you've been feeling this all along?"

"For the past couple of years, for sure."

"Why didn't you say something to me?"

Scott shrugged. "You've been trying to be Pop ever since you were a little kid. I figured that sooner or later, you'd take a look around and see that Pop is Pop, I'm me, and you're you."

Why was it, Kevin wondered, that the most obvious things were often the toughest to grasp?

JUST BEFORE SIX IN THE morning, Lisa stood at Jamie's bedside watching her child sleep. Tonight was the Thanksgiving pageant, and she knew that she had much to be thankful for. She had her son, safe and secure in the knowledge that he was loved. She had her parents and her friends. She smoothed Jamie's covers, let her gaze skip the yellow truck that rested at his feet, and left her son to his dreams for just a little while longer.

Intent on starting her day, Lisa went into the bathroom and turned on the shower. Once the water's temperature was as stingingly hot as she liked it, she peeled off her nightgown, stepped under the flow, pulled the curtain, and shut herself away from the world.

During their marriage, she had hardly viewed James as a saint. He'd had his shortcomings, but had offered his compensations, too. Before they'd moved back to her hometown, they'd had their adventures, backpacking across Europe, he writing while she worked in cafés for spending money. They'd laughed, made love and done whatever they'd wanted to.

But even back then, he'd known how to be quietly hurtful, throwing sharp verbal darts, eroding her self-confidence so subtly that she hadn't even noticed its disappearance until long after it had gone. About now, she resented him for that. Deeply.

James had been five years older than she. Despite that chronological measurement, in so many ways he'd still been a rash adolescent. Had she not married him, he would have been a blast to travel with…for about six months. Had they never had Jamie, he would have kept that pampered central role in their lives. But Jamie had come along, and James hadn't been willing—or maybe even able—to step up. And grow up.

Lisa sluiced her hair back against her head as the water pelted her. She didn't hate James. But as she thought about all that she'd done alone, she would have loved to have him back just long enough to tell him what she thought of his total opt-out of their lives.

Because there was no one there to watch her, no one there to judge, she allowed herself to own her anger, to make it hers and let it burn hotter and higher. She closed her eyes and envisioned grabbing James and shaking him. No, she would tackle him and rub his nose in what he'd done, how he'd hurt her. *Bad James! Naughty James!*

What? Had she finally lost it?

She laughed, first tentatively and then straight from the gut at the total craziness of her thoughts. And then she laughed because she was standing in her shower laughing like a loon. Then finally, she cried.

Hot water eventually ran warm, and then cool. Before she made a shivering wreck of herself, Lisa turned off the shower, dried off with the thick towel that Kevin had given her, and let the day draw her forward.

Chapter Fourteen

By six that evening, Jamie had been delivered backstage in his pilgrim best, and Lisa and Courtney were back out front scanning the crowd in the auditorium's reception area for Suz. Lisa's mom and dad had been accounted for, but were occupied making their social rounds. Lisa was cool with that, as one more sad shake of her mother's head was going to send her round the bend. And for this evening, at least, she was determined to hold it together.

Just then, a hand settled on her shoulder. She permitted herself a brief fantasy that it would be Kevin. It wasn't, of course. Lisa recognized one of the dads she'd seen working on Kevin's set building crew.

"Hi, John," she said.

He distractedly returned her greeting before asking, "Is Kevin here?"

"No," Lisa replied. "He couldn't make it."

She ignored Courtney's rather inelegant snort.

"Think you might be able to reach him?" John asked.

"Sorry, but he's on the road, so I don't think so. Is something wrong with the set?"

"No, the set's great, but we're having a little issue with Jamie."

Lisa automatically began heading toward the backstage area, but the milling crowd was too thick to move quickly. "Why didn't you just say so?"

"Well, he's not asking for you," John replied. "He's asking for Kevin."

"Sorry, I'm all that's available."

"Almost all," Courtney said.

John looked at the two of them, then nodded. "I guess you'll have to do."

Nice.

In just a few moments, they were down a quiet corridor and to the backstage area, and then the packed dressing room. Pilgrims, Native Americans and children dressed as woodland creatures were everywhere. Lisa didn't see Jamie, though.

"Where is…" She trailed off when she saw a very dear and familiar little boy standing behind a barricade of three folding chairs against a wall.

"He closed himself in when we told him it was time to line up," John said.

Lisa hurried over to her son, who was one pale pilgrim, indeed. She could tell that he'd been crying, and now he was doing his best to pretend that no one was around him.

"What's up, sweetie?" she asked. "Are you feeling okay?"

She hoped he wasn't about to have another holiday ruined by the flu.

"I'm not going," he said in a tight voice. "Don't wanna be a pilgrim."

Ah, stage fright. She remembered it well.

"I know it looks scary with all the people out there," she said. "Just look at your friends with you on the stage and—"

Jamie wiped his nose with the back of his hand. "Want Kevin."

"Honey, you know Kevin had to leave."

He started sniffling again. "Want *Kev-iiiin!* He's my daddy!"

At the sound of his heartache, Lisa wanted to cry, too. "Honey, he's your friend, but you know he's not your daddy, right?"

"He helped with the daddies. Those daddies are here. Won't go without *my* daddy."

"Jamie—"

She wasn't quite sure what she'd been about to say, but Courtney's steadying hand on her shoulder had silenced her. There was nothing she *could* say, except she'd screwed up and stolen her son's chosen measure of security.

"He's my Thanksgiving daddy. Not going." Jamie sat cross-legged behind his wall of chairs. "Can't make me."

Lisa supposed she could, though it didn't seem the best idea. Not that she'd been exactly in top form when it came to bright ideas lately.

"Let me," Courtney said softly enough that it wouldn't carry.

"Might as well," Lisa said. "I'm striking out."

Courtney sat on one of the chairs in front of Jamie.

"You know what's in this big purse of mine?" she asked him, patting the enormous red bag.

"Not Kevin," he said flatly, and Courtney laughed.

"No, my brother wouldn't fit in there, would he?"

Jamie shook his head.

"But a movie camera docs. Kevin wished he could be here, but he promised our daddy that he'd go to Arizona to see him. He didn't forget about you, though. He'd never do that. He asked me to make a movie of your show so he could see it right away."

Jamie sat up. "He did?"

Courtney nodded. "Yes, and he'd be very sad if he watched the movie and couldn't find you in it. You don't want that, do you?"

"No," he tentatively replied.

"Then how about you go out there and let me make a really good movie to send to Kevin?"

Jamie stood, and Lisa released the breath she hadn't even realized she'd been holding.

"'Kay," he said. "But it's no fair. Want Kevin."

With either of those points Lisa couldn't argue.

BY THE TIME JAMIE WAS settled in line with the other students, the audience had already taken their seats. Lisa spotted Suz standing and looking toward the back of the room. She waved and pointed to two seats she'd apparently saved. Lisa and Courtney made it down to the rest of the group just as the curtain rose.

"Wow," Courtney murmured. "Talk about not being able to see the forest for the trees. Kevin and Jamie's group made all of those?"

Lisa nodded. "Every last one."

"Pity he couldn't be here to see them," her mother leaned across Suz to comment.

Lisa watched out of the corner of her eye as her dad simultaneously drew her mom back and gave her a comforting pat. Lisa could have used one of those. She'd felt dreadful all day, as though she was on the brink of something even bigger and unhappier than the emotions that had washed over her in the shower this morning. She'd pushed away the feeling while at work and when getting Jamie ready. Now, though, as the lights dimmed and the sound of a single, plaintive flute drifted over the audience, she could hold it back no longer.

She sat back in her seat and tried to focus on the children dressed as deer weaving between the trees more or less in time to the music. She couldn't seem to move her attention from those trees, though. Those solid, totally upright and eminently trustworthy trees. Okay, so she wasn't thinking so much of the trees as she was of their creator.

He'd been in front of her all these years, and yet she had never seen the truth of him. Now she could see him so very clearly—his rock-steady patience, his way of bringing out the best in everyone, even four-year-olds building trees—but he no longer wanted to see her. She'd been so lost in her own insecurities, so wrapped up in the ghost of a relationship that no longer existed, that she'd pushed away the one man who'd wanted to help her find her way home.

James had been gone for years, and still she'd been using him as an excuse to fend off intimacy. This had been her issue, not James's, God rest him, and definitely not Kevin's. Oh, she'd tried mightily to force Kevin into the role of James, but deep inside she'd known that he was different. And she'd begun to learn that she was no longer the same overwhelmed and lonely girl she'd once been. If she'd trusted herself—trusted Kevin—life would have been amazing.

Lisa glanced up at the stage through a sheen of tears that made her vision waver and dance. Little Native Americans and pilgrims had joined in the slow dance. She spotted Jamie, who looked serious and proud, chin held high. The children wove around each other, far more adept at finding the proper pathway than she'd ever been.

Now she saw it: the forest, the trees, what she wanted, and how she'd never again push away a man in order to avoid having him turn away all on his own.

A hand settled over hers, where she'd been gripping the armrest of the auditorium chair.

"It will be okay," Courtney whispered.

And it would.

But it never would be *amazing* again.

Chapter Fifteen

"Okay, I'm here," Courtney announced early Thanksgiving morning as she entered Shortbread Cottage's kitchen. "Give me a job, but make it simple. Kids I can handle, but I stink as a cook. The relish tray, maybe. I can open pickle jars with the best of 'em."

From her post at the prep counter, Lisa smiled at her friend's boundless enthusiasm—and honesty. Today wouldn't be the stuff of lifelong memories, but it would be survivable, thanks to friends and family.

"Go for it," she said to Courtney. "And one word of advice—keep out of my mom's way. She has a spreadsheet three pages long, both color-coded and cross-indexed with a seating chart. Suz is trying to keep her cut off from the rest of us, but you know Mom…"

"I sure do," Courtney said with a laugh.

Jamie came running from the living room into the kitchen. "Miss Courtney! Miss Courtney!" He flung himself at his babysitter, who bent down to accept his hug. "Did you bring Kevin? Did you?"

Despite the arrow to her heart, Lisa kept a pleasant expression on her face.

"No, Jamie," Courtney said. "Kevin's still with our mom and dad. But I'm here, and we'll think up something fun to do. Promise!"

Jamie gave Courtney a highly skeptical look. Lisa would have laughed if she didn't ache so much. It was bad enough that she'd hurt herself, but to hurt her son was exponentially worse.

"I'm gonna go color," Jamie announced grumpily, and left the kitchen for the private part of their home.

Lisa sighed. "I'm sorry. Every time he asks, I tell him that Kevin's gone for the winter, but hope springs eternal and all that."

"It's okay. I've been slighted by more men than young Master Jamie. So how are you doing?"

Lisa looked down at the onion she was chopping. "Other than yet another freakish crying jag, I'm holding my own."

"That's a start, I guess. You know Kevin's—"

Lisa shook her head. "Could we save that topic for another day? I've had enough of crying."

"Says the woman chopping the onions," Courtney replied. "But I won't bring him up until you want me to."

Lisa chopped harder, and Courtney took the hint.

"Okay, no Kevin talk. So how many people are we expecting?" she asked.

"The final tally is twenty-five," announced Lisa's mother, who had just entered the kitchen from the café.

"Of course there are those who don't quite get around to delivering an RSVP, so we're setting for thirty. I've brought the silver from home. Courtney, you may give it a final polish before we set the tables."

Courtney opened her mouth and then closed it, rather like a fish gasping for air. Lisa decided to rescue her.

"Sorry, Mom. I've already put Court on pickle duty. And I'm willing to bet the silver's plenty shiny without another polish."

"Pickle duty," her mother muttered, then marched from the room.

"You'll find the pickles and olives in the pantry cupboard, and the relish trays right here to my left," Lisa directed. "And I'd advise you to take your time opening those jars. We have five hours until dinner, and much heirloom silver awaits."

"I'll make each pickle count," Courtney promised.

They worked in silence for a few minutes. But as each second passed, the temptation to speak of Kevin grew stronger. If she said his name, he'd no longer be the elephant in the middle of the kitchen.

"So what does your family do for Thanksgiving down there in Arizona?" Lisa asked.

Courtney glanced over at her. "Thought you didn't want to talk about Kevin."

"This isn't about Kevin, specifically," she hedged. "I'm just making small talk."

Which was hooey. She just wanted to feel some connection to the man she missed so deeply.

"Okay," Courtney said in a dangerously perky tone. "Well, when we have Thanksgiving down in Carefree, *Kevin* gets up early to golf eighteen holes with Dad. And then after that, *Kevin* comes back and sets up the turkey fryer in the driveway. Scott and *Kevin* like fried turkey, but the rest of us like the traditional overroasted bird, so we cook two. We eat dinner around three, and then Scott, Mike, Dad and *Kevin* watch football while Mom and I start planning our Christmas shopping route for the next day. *Kevin* isn't much for television, so he usually ends up challenging Mike to a game of horse at the basketball court down the road. How's that? Enough Decker family trivia?"

Lisa chopped her onions harder, not caring if she'd gone from chop to mince to totally pulverized and useless in their texture. Anything to hide the tears.

Courtney sighed and set down the jar of gherkins she'd been doling into the three relish trays. She walked to Lisa, hand extended.

"Want to give me the knife before you work your way through the countertop?" she asked.

Defeated, Lisa set the knife aside.

"Is it okay if I hug you?"

Lisa nodded. "I think it might be mandatory."

As Courtney wrapped her in her arms for a tough-love hug, Lisa tried to back off on the tears.

"Here's a novel thought," Courtney said after they'd stepped out of their embrace. "If you miss him, call him."

"But he hasn't called me."

Her friend rolled her eyes. "And so? What are you, fourteen? If he doesn't call, you can't pick up the phone?"

"I don't know what I'd say to him."

"What do you want to say to him?"

"That I love him. That I'm sorry I freaked out on him. That I'll do my best not to treat him like Satan's spawn ever again." She shrugged, feeling kind of embarrassed that she'd just admitted her lunacy to Kevin's sister. "All of that...or Happy Thanksgiving."

Courtney smiled. "I'm sure both messages would be welcome, but one a little more than the other."

"Yeah, well, it's easier to say it to you than to him."

"But the payoff is better if you say it to him."

"Or worse. Way worse. What if he doesn't care anymore? What if he's had enough and just wants some girl who's never had a baby, never been married...never been quite so messed up?"

Courtney shook her head. "What, and miss all the excitement?"

"Not funny," Lisa said.

"I know. Seriously, Lisa, when he started acting all proprietary about you, I thought maybe he was seeing you as some sort of wounded bird he could take care of. He's great at that...taking care of others. I think it helps him not focus on the stuff in his life that's not quite together. But whatever. I'm no one to talk. Anyway, I started watching you two, and I realized that he loves you. Really, totally loves you. Otherwise, he wouldn't have been acting so quiet and weird before he and Scott left."

"I'm sorry. I never wanted to hurt him."

"Wrong audience. Tell him."

Lisa looked at the clock on the kitchen wall. "It's too early, just after seven down there. He'll—"

"Maybe he'll be out golfing with my dad, and pick up your message later. Then you don't have the pressure of talking to him right this second. *Call* him."

She looked at her friend, thought of her son, and listened to her mother's laughter coming from the café. All of this would still be here even if Kevin told her there was no going back. If she'd lost him, she had, and she would survive. But if she hadn't lost him, and she could grab this last ingredient for happiness...

"Take over the onions," she said to Courtney. "I've got some explaining to do."

KEVIN LOOKED AT HIS ringing cell phone, where it sat plugged into the charger on the console of his truck. He could answer it, or he could just keep on driving and asking himself why he was where he was, and what he thought it would gain him. He could be golfing with Pop, but no. He could be having coffee with Mom, but no. Instead, here he was...in his damn truck again.

Scott had already called twice this morning with turkey fryer prep questions, and Kevin would bet that this was him with yet another detail to be picked apart. Who'd have thought that Scott was such a detail guy, after all?

And who else would be calling him? Kevin wondered. He'd managed to annoy both his mom and dad within hours of arriving in Carefree. He supposed it could have something to do with his pretty testy mood. The farther he'd gotten from Davenport, the more restless he'd become.

Without taking his dry and sleep-deprived eyes from the road, Kevin flipped open the phone and said, "Put whatever herbs you want under the skin. Use whatever brand of oil you like. But the bottom line is that you just stick the dead bird in the fryer and cook the hell out of it, okay?"

"I…ah… Okay, then," said a female voice.

Kevin's heart rolled over. *"Lisa?"*

"Um, yes?"

Even though he was in a quiet residential area, he looked to his right, hit his turn signal, and pulled to the side of the road. Driving while talking was dangerous enough. Driving while talking to Lisa, even more so, when all he wanted was to hear her voice and know that even if he wasn't with her, she was okay.

"You still there?" he asked.

"Yes."

"Sorry about the weird greeting. I thought you were Scott."

"I see." She drew in an audible breath, and Kevin wished he could make this easier for her. "How's… how's Thanksgiving going for you?"

"Interesting," he replied. Even more so by the second.

"Well, I guess interesting can be good."

"Yes," he agreed. "How's your Thanksgiving shaping up?"

"Nice, I think. Your sister is here, helping me get ready. My mom, too. But that's not why I called…"

He didn't think that a current events report had been, but he also didn't want to set his hopes too high.

"I called to say I'm sorry," she said. "I made a mess of things. I should have had faith in you…in us."

He closed his eyes as relief washed over him. "We both made a mess of things."

He'd been an idiot to take off to Arizona simply because she'd stepped on his pride. His patience, the one thing he usually had in surplus, had deserted him. With distance came perspective, though. He knew now that she'd been scared that night. He should have just let it be, but he'd pushed her. Now here he was, and there she was…

One short block away.

"Look," Lisa said. "I appreciate your saying that, but you were right. I was stuck in some sort of endless loop that replayed all the things James ever said that were wrong about me, and none of the things I knew were right."

He had to kiss her…now.

Kevin turned off his truck and pulled his keys from the ignition. After he'd exited, he closed the door as quietly as he could. Apparently not quietly enough, because she asked, "What was that?"

He winced. "Sorry, I'm just banging around in Pop's garage. Scott's at the market picking up some things for the turkey that I forgot yesterday, and I'm trying to get the fryer set up."

"Oh, okay. It sounded like a car door or something dropping."

"The fryer stand," he said. All in all, he was pleased with his fabrication on the fly.

"So long as you're okay."

"Doing great," he said as he strolled past, first, Amanda's BMW and then his sister's day care van.

"Maybe I should call you back," Lisa said. "You sound pretty busy."

"No," he replied, but the word came out more harshly than he'd intended.

He needed this connection; he needed her on the line until he had her in his arms. Her silence cued him in to the fact that she might have taken his response the wrong way, though.

"What I meant was let's talk. I've missed the sound of your voice, Lisa."

THE LIST OF THINGS THAT LISA had missed about Kevin was endless. For starters, there was his dimple when he smiled, not to mention his smile. She'd missed the way Jamie brightened when he came into a room, and she'd missed that rush of love that shot through her when she saw him, too. And most of all, she'd missed the sense that when the two of them were together, it would always be good…no matter what complications life threw their way.

"I've missed you, too," she said, since the rest of it was just too personal to be blurting in front of Jamie, Courtney, Suz and her mom, who had all gathered in the kitchen to watch her, as though this call was more entertaining than a Thanksgiving parade. She walked past them into the café, and issued a firm command of *stay* when she caught them creeping toward her.

"Stay?" Kevin asked. "You didn't get Jamie a puppy, did you?"

She laughed. "No. I might be crazy in what I take on, but I'm not that crazy." And just because she wanted time to build her courage before she moved on to the serious stuff, she asked, "How's the weather down there?"

He was silent for a beat, then said, "Cool. Definitely cool for Carefree."

"Bummer," she said.

"How is it where you are?"

"I don't know," she said. "I haven't even been outside today, which is weird, you know? With Jamie, I'm always going outside."

"Careful. You don't want to break a streak like that. You might as well step outside and check it out, don't you think?"

Lisa absently dusted off the top of the espresso machine and looked at the slightly coffee-splattered instructions taped to the wall next to it. She really needed to print out a clean sheet.

"I'm kind of liking the inside option, but thanks," she said.

"Really, I think you want to turn around, go to the café door and check out the weather."

He'd spoken as though she might be just the tiniest bit dense, but she would put that objection aside because another matter was troubling her.

"How do you know where I—"

Her question was cut short by a squeal from Jamie, who danced in the kitchen door. Courtney was holding him back, a broad grin on her face.

Then Lisa heard a rapping sound….

Slowly, she turned, wishing, hoping, and also knowing it to be true: the most amazing man in the whole, wide world stood outside her door, waiting for her to love him. And because she had grown to be a wise, wise woman, this time, she would let him in.

* * * * *

*Celebrate 60 years of pure reading pleasure
with Harlequin®!*

To commemorate the event, Silhouette Special
Edition invites you to Ashley O'Ballivan's bed-
and-breakfast in the small town of Stone Creek.
The beautiful innkeeper will have her hands full
caring for her old flame Jack McCall. He's on the
run and recovering from a mysterious illness, but
that won't stop him from trying to win Ashley back.

*Enjoy an exclusive glimpse of Linda Lael Miller's
AT HOME IN STONE CREEK
Available in November 2009 from
Silhouette Special Edition®*

The helicopter swung abruptly sideways in a dizzying arch, setting Jack McCall's fever-ravaged brain spinning.

His friend's voice sounded tinny, coming through the earphones. "You belong in a hospital," he said. "Not some backwater bed-and-breakfast."

All Jack really knew about the virus raging through his system was that it wasn't contagious, and there was no known treatment for it besides a lot of rest and quiet. "I don't like hospitals," he responded, hoping he sounded like his normal self. "They're full of sick people."

Vince Griffin chuckled but it was a dry sound, rough at the edges. "What's in Stone Creek, Arizona?" he asked. "Besides a whole lot of nothin'?"

Ashley O'Ballivan was in Stone Creek, and she was a whole lot of somethin', but Jack had neither the strength nor the inclination to explain. After the way he'd ducked out six months before, he didn't expect a welcome, knew he didn't deserve one. But Ashley, being Ashley, would take him in whatever her misgivings.

He had to get to Ashley; he'd be all right.

He closed his eyes, letting the fever swallow him.

There was no telling how much time had passed when he became aware of the chopper blades slowing overhead. Dimly, he saw the private ambulance waiting on the airfield outside of Stone Creek; it seemed that twilight had descended.

Jack sighed with relief. His clothes felt clammy against his flesh. His teeth began to chatter as two figures unloaded a gurney from the back of the ambulance and waited for the blades to stop.

"Great," Vince remarked, unsnapping his seat belt. "Those two look like volunteers, not real EMTs."

The chopper bounced sickeningly on its runners, and Vince, with a shake of his head, pushed open his door and jumped to the ground, head down.

Jack waited, wondering if he'd be able to stand on his own. After fumbling unsuccessfully with the buckle on his seat belt, he decided not.

When it was safe the EMTs approached, following Vince, who opened Jack's door.

His old friend Tanner Quinn stepped around Vince, his grin not quite reaching his eyes.

"You look like hell warmed over," he told Jack cheerfully.

"Since when are you an EMT?" Jack retorted.

Tanner reached in, wedged a shoulder under Jack's right arm and hauled him out of the chopper. His knees immediately buckled, and Vince stepped up, supporting him on the other side.

"In a place like Stone Creek," Tanner replied, "everybody helps out."

They reached the wheeled gurney, and Jack found himself on his back.

Tanner and the second man strapped him down, a process that brought back a few bad memories.

"Is there even a hospital in this place?" Vince asked irritably from somewhere in the night.

"There's a pretty good clinic over in Indian Rock," Tanner answered easily, "and it isn't far to Flagstaff." He paused to help his buddy hoist Jack and the gurney into the back of the ambulance. "You're in good hands, Jack. My wife is the best veterinarian in the state."

Jack laughed raggedly at that.

Vince muttered a curse.

Tanner climbed into the back beside him, perched on some kind of fold-down seat. The other man shut the doors.

"You in any pain?" Tanner said as his partner climbed into the driver's seat and started the engine.

"No." Jack looked up at his oldest and closest friend and wished he'd listened to Vince. Ever since he'd come down with the virus—a week after snatching a five-year-old girl back from her non-custodial parent, a small-time Colombian drug dealer—he hadn't been able to think about anyone or anything but Ashley. When he *could* think, anyway.

Now, in one of the first clearheaded moments he'd experienced since checking himself out of Bethesda the day before, he realized he might be making a major mistake. Not by facing Ashley—he owed her that much and a lot more. No, he could be putting her in danger, putting Tanner and his daughter and his pregnant wife in danger, too.

"I shouldn't have come here," he said, keeping his voice low.

Tanner shook his head, his jaw clamped down hard as though he was irritated by Jack's statement.

"This is where you belong," Tanner insisted. "If you'd had sense enough to know that six months ago, old buddy, when you bailed on Ashley without so much as a fare-thee-well, you wouldn't be in this mess."

Ashley. The name had run through his mind a million times in those six months, but hearing somebody say it out loud was like having a fist close around his insides and squeeze hard.

Jack couldn't speak.

Tanner didn't press for further conversation.

The ambulance bumped over country roads, finally hitting smooth blacktop.

"Here we are," Tanner said. "Ashley's place."

* * * * *

Will Jack be able to patch things up with Ashley,
or will his past put the woman he loves in harm's way?
Find out in
AT HOME IN STONE CREEK
by Linda Lael Miller
Available November 2009 from
Silhouette Special Edition®

Copyright © 2009 by Linda Lael Miller

This November,
Silhouette Special Edition®
brings you

NEW YORK TIMES
BESTSELLING AUTHOR

LINDA LAEL MILLER

At Home in
Stone Creek

*Available in November
wherever books are sold.*

Visit Silhouette Books at www.eHarlequin.com

SSELLM60BPA

HARLEQUIN
Ambassadors

Want to share your passion for reading Harlequin® Books?

Become a Harlequin Ambassador!

Harlequin Ambassadors are a group of passionate and well-connected readers who are willing to share their joy of reading Harlequin® books with family and friends.

You'll be sent all the tools you need to spark great conversation, including free books!

All we ask is that you share the romance with your friends and family!

You'll also be invited to have a say in new book ideas and exchange opinions with women just like you!

To see if you qualify* to be a Harlequin Ambassador, please visit www.HarlequinAmbassadors.com.

*Please note that not everyone who applies to be a Harlequin Ambassador will qualify. For more information please visit www.HarlequinAmbassadors.com.

Thank you for your participation.

BAP09BPA

Romantic
SUSPENSE

Sparked by Danger,
Fueled by Passion.

Blackout
At Christmas

Beth Cornelison,
Sharron McClellan,
Jennifer Morey

What happens when a major blackout shuts down the entire Western seaboard on Christmas Eve? Follow stories of danger, intrigue and romance as three women learn to trust their instincts to survive and open their hearts to the love that unexpectedly comes their way.

Available November
wherever books are sold.

Visit Silhouette Books at www.eHarlequin.com

SRS27653

HARLEQUIN® Romance®

This November,
queen of the rugged rancher

PATRICIA THAYER

teams up with

DONNA ALWARD

to bring you an extra-special treat
this holiday season—

two romantic stories
in one book!

Join sisters Amelia and Kelley for Christmas at
Rocking H Ranch where these feisty cowgirls swap
presents for proposals, mistletoe for marriage and
experience the unbeatable rush of falling in love!

Available in November wherever books are sold.

www.eHarlequin.com

HR17619

REQUEST YOUR FREE BOOKS!

2 FREE NOVELS PLUS 2 FREE GIFTS!

HARLEQUIN®

American ★ Romance®

Love, Home & Happiness!

YES! Please send me 2 FREE Harlequin® American Romance® novels and my 2 FREE gifts (gifts are worth about $10). After receiving them, if I don't wish to receive any more books, I can return the shipping statement marked "cancel." If I don't cancel, I will receive 4 brand-new novels every month and be billed just $4.24 per book in the U.S. or $4.99 per book in Canada.* That's a savings of close to 15% off the cover price! It's quite a bargain! Shipping and handling is just 50¢ per book. I understand that accepting the 2 free books and gifts places me under no obligation to buy anything. I can always return a shipment and cancel at any time. Even if I never buy another book from Harlequin, the two free books and gifts are mine to keep forever.

154 HDN E4DS 354 HDN E4D4

Name	(PLEASE PRINT)	
Address		Apt. #
City	State/Prov.	Zip/Postal Code

Signature (if under 18, a parent or guardian must sign)

Mail to the **Harlequin Reader Service:**
IN U.S.A.: P.O. Box 1867, Buffalo, NY 14240-1867
IN CANADA: P.O. Box 609, Fort Erie, Ontario L2A 5X3

Not valid to current subscribers of Harlequin® American Romance® books.

Want to try two free books from another line?
Call 1-800-873-8635 or visit www.morefreebooks.com.

* Terms and prices subject to change without notice. Prices do not include applicable taxes. N.Y. residents add applicable sales tax. Canadian residents will be charged applicable provincial taxes and GST. Offer not valid in Quebec. This offer is limited to one order per household. All orders subject to approval. Credit or debit balances in a customer's account(s) may be offset by any other outstanding balance owed by or to the customer. Please allow 4 to 6 weeks for delivery. Offer available while quantities last.

Your Privacy: Harlequin is committed to protecting your privacy. Our Privacy Policy is available online at www.eHarlequin.com or upon request from the Reader Service. From time to time we make our lists of customers available to reputable third parties who may have a product or service of interest to you. If you would prefer we not share your name and address, please check here. ☐

HAR09R2

NEW YORK TIMES BESTSELLING AUTHORS

DEBBIE MACOMBER
SHERRYL WOODS
ROBYN CARR

Celebrate the holidays
with three stories
from your
favorite authors.

"Silver Bells" by Debbie Macomber
In this classic story, Debbie brings those Manning men and
Manning sisters home for a mistletoe marriage when a single
dad finally says "I do."

"The Perfect Holiday" by Sherryl Woods
Will bachelor Trace Franklin become a groom-to-be by
Christmastime? He sure will...if Savannah Holiday's Aunt
Mae has anything to do with it.

"Under the Christmas Tree" by Robyn Carr
When the folks of Virgin River discover a box of adorable
puppies under the town's Christmas tree they call on local vet
Nathaniel Jensen for help. But it's his budding romance with
Annie McCarty that really has tongues—and tails—wagging!

That Holiday Feeling

MIRA®

Available September 29 wherever books are sold!

www.MIRABooks.com

MV2837

HARLEQUIN®

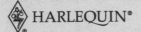
American ★ Romance®

COMING NEXT MONTH
Available November 10, 2009

#1281 THE FIREMAN'S CHRISTMAS by Meg Lacey
Men Made in America

Danny Santori is a single dad with four kids, and Tessa Doherty has her own two children to raise. In desperation, the small-town neighbors turn to each other for shared babysitting duties. With six kids and their busy careers, who's got time for the scorching romance heating up between them?

#1282 THE COWBOY FROM CHRISTMAS PAST by Tina Leonard

Finding a baby on his porch in the middle of a snowstorm could be Dillinger Kent's Christmas miracle. Especially when the 1892 gunslinger is propelled into present-day Dallas...and meets Auburn McGinnis. The perfume heiress accepts him for who he is in spite of the hundred-plus years between them. Has the widowed cowboy found what he's been looking for? A love that transcends time?

#1283 COLORADO CHRISTMAS by C. C. Coburn
The O'Malley Men

Becky McBride, judge and single mom, will admit that Spruce Lake, Colorado, looks just like a Christmas card. But Becky has her doubts about the town. Especially when a good-looking rogue named Will O'Malley seems intent on making her fall in love with Spruce Lake *and* with him...despite all her plans to the contrary!

#1284 A HOLIDAY TO REMEMBER by Lynnette Kent

The moment Jayne Thomas opened the door, Chris Hammond knew—he'd found the childhood sweetheart he'd loved and lost twelve years ago. Only, she doesn't know *him* at all. If she can't remember a past that he'll never forget, then Chris must love Jayne for the woman she's become, or risk losing her again....

www.eHarlequin.com

HARCNMBPA1009